# Murder
## on Wilson Street

Faye Duncan

Murder on Wilson Street
Faye Duncan

Published June 2016
Little Creek Books
Imprint of Jan-Carol Publishing, Inc.
Cover Design: Oxana Barsukova
Cover Illustration: Bob. J. Elson


ISBN: 978-1-939289-98-8
Library of Congress Control Number: 2016944724

You may contact the publisher:
Jan-Carol Publishing, Inc.
PO Box 701
Johnson City, TN 37605
publisher@jancarolpublishing.com
jancarolpublishing.com

*

*For TJ, who went away too soon.*
*May your gentle soul rest in peace.*

*

# A Letter to the Reader

The original idea for this story came to me in 2006, when I was living in a brownstone in Koreatown with a long dark hallway and apartment doors numbering more than the eye could count...if you've ever lived anywhere near Downtown LA, you probably know exactly what I'm talking about.

This was my very first place in LA. From the sleeping homeless man who blocked the door, to the police visits, to the shopping carts pushed in front of my window at any hour of the day, I could not stop thinking that I had landed inside Paul Auster's story: *In the Country of Lost Things.*

My choice to create a series which showcases the City of Pasadena came much later.

Now, you may wonder how it is possible that a little mystery would take almost ten years to complete. But if you have a writer's mind like I do, you know how hard it is to focus on just one project.

So bear with me. I hope you enjoy my little piece about this "haughty city."

– Faye

# Acknowledgements

I would like to thank my friend Lorna for the support as a fellow writer, for your intelligent and open-minded views on novel writing, the invaluable editing help, and just for being a great friend.

Also, thank you to my friend Ben for all your valuable insights and constructive criticism. It takes a gentle soul to understand a gentle soul. And while I am definitely not a Tolstoy, I know we both appreciate the slogan: "It's progress, not perfection!"

Thank you also to my team of publishers and editors. Everyone from Jan-Carol Publishing, Inc. has been incredibly encouraging and supportive. I feel I have finally found the type of support I have been looking for so long.

Thank you, also, to all my other friends who provided me with their valuable thoughts and ideas.

# Table of Contents

# Driving to the Shop

It was just another day in Emma Robinson's solitary life. She was on her way to work in her leased metallic-gold 2007 Toyota Camry when a shiny black Honda Acura cut her off on the entry ramp to 110 South, heading toward Downtown L.A. The Honda wore a bra over its nose. Emma loathed the concept. The idea of a bra on a car made her feel naked.

*Darn that driver!* Emma almost gave him the middle finger through the car window. Then she thought better of it. Traffic was heavy at this hour; it was 7:30 AM, and Ray was expecting her yesterday. She was running a quick errand on his behalf before work, and didn't want to risk being later than she already was because she got in trouble with some dude on the road.

Ray had sent her out to buy new ribbon spool for his Underwood typewriter. Although he'd mastered all newer technologies like a pro, he remained attached to some of their most useless predecessors. One of these attachments was his portable Underwood typewriter, with Persian key tops. It had traveled with him when he left Tehran to evade the Iranian massacre, in 1988. Ray had lost a lot on the road, but the typewriter and Ray had remained an inseparable pair. When Emma once asked him why he used a typewriter, he explained in a frenzy that his thoughts flowed better when he saw them on a piece of paper rather than on a computer screen, so he stuck to it. For Emma, on the other hand, her employer was designated as a mad eccentric from day one.

Emma's job was to translate his texts from Farsi, a language skill that she had acquired in her linguistics studies at Columbia University. It wasn't enough that she had to decipher meaning from a difficult foreign language; oh, no, he had to type it on *that* old thing, which the youth of today had probably never even heard about. At least she didn't have to decipher the content from handwritten notes, she consoled herself. It was time now to get out of her head and find that store. Traffic was hell in L.A. at the wrong time in the morning.

Of course, Emma had made sure on Friday night before she left for the weekend that somebody would be at the store when she arrived on Monday morning. Small, specialized stores like that didn't open until the late morning hours. And so, like many of us, Emma was just another Angelino among millions, working incognito for too many hours to help Ray's booming career boom some more, but never her own.

Emma dreaded the next phone conversation with her mother, who kept reminding her of the enormous salary her father had made. She was relieved that she didn't have to share her struggles with her father, in a way. He had passed away only a few months before she left New York for L.A. God bless his caring soul.

Ray had hired her to transcribe his theoretical treatments *Thoughts and Sketches about the Judeo-Islamic conflict in the Middle East*, which he had started early on in his career, years before he won the Nobel Prize for *Flames of Passion* in 2006, a tacky romance between a Hezbollah soldier and a Jewish schoolteacher. It was only now, after his bestselling novel had turned into a smash hit, that he found time to continue his *Thoughts*. Even so, with his position as a lecturer on Contemporary Middle Eastern Politics in the Social Sciences Department at Caltech, with a wife and two children, he only had so much time to work on his projects. It had been wise of him to hire her, Emma knew. Also, despite the great traffic stress, she was able to relax a bit.

Emma was just trying to pull into a parking place on Figueroa Street when her smartphone rang. She checked her display: Ray West. Really? It wasn't even 8:00 AM yet. She answered anyway.

"Yes? Hello, this is Emma," she said, with the phone stuck between her shoulder and her chin. She was backing into a parallel space. Her Bluetooth was still in the shop, waiting for her to purchase it. She didn't give a hoot about all that technology, and hoped a cop wouldn't see her.

"Emma, I'm sorry for disturbing you so early," Ray said with his sweet Persian accent. Maybe it was just her, but his accent somehow reminded her of the clumsy enunciation of a young child. It made her smile every time she heard it. Only today, it wouldn't be more than a ghost of a smile.

"No problem!" Emma denied, and nearly hit the car behind her with the bumper. She dropped her phone and switched into forward gear. Then she picked up the phone again.

"There has been a terrible accident here," Emma barely heard Ray say, as if from a distance. She decided to put the phone in speaker mode.

"What are you saying, Ray? I'm sorry; I'm going to the store, and trying to park my car."

"It looks like somebody attacked Miss Woodbridge. Katie found her body in the door, before she left for work this morning. The police are here now. I thought I'd warn you before you come back here. I know you're on the way to the typewriter shop, right?"

Emma turned the motor off.

"What? Aunt Nettie?"

"Yes, Emma. Natalie Woodbridge. I know you cared a lot about her."

"Aunt Nettie is dead?"

"I'm afraid there's nothing that can be done," Ray said.

"But, but...I don't understand! How could anyone harm such a friendly old lady?"

"I don't know, Emma. Right now, I don't think that anybody knows. Nevertheless, I thought I would tell you before the police did. They are all over the place here."

"I appreciate it, Ray."

"Just do what you need to do, and be sure to drive home safely. Okay, Emma?"

"Okay. I'll talk to you later, I guess." Emma hung up.

It was barely eight o'clock on Monday morning, and Emma was feeling devastated.

***

Carefully, Emma grabbed the long ends of the beige trench coat that covered her lean body as she stepped out of the car to make sure she wouldn't trip over a pothole. The busy shopping street was in utter neglect. "No means is too sophisticated for the Los Angeles police to charge the citizens for parking," Emma remarked, astounded, as she slid her Citibank MasterCard into a high-tech parking meter equipped with a card reader. *They'd be better off doing something about the morals of their citizens*, Emma thought, minding the puddles of broken glass along the sidewalks, the remainders of a night's break-in. Involuntarily, her mind wandered back to Aunt Nettie, whom she had only said goodbye to a few hours ago, after she had taken her to the movie theater. There was no time for this now, though. Emma needed to get to the shop.

Checking left and right that no one was coming, she crossed the street to where she assumed the typewriter shop was located. She gently stroked the side of her head—Emma was wearing her thick, blonde hair in an elegant bun today, and she wanted to make sure the drive hadn't taken it all apart. The bun was usually the next best solution to a ponytail, to tame her full head of blonde chaos. It gave her look the notch of elegance that she'd wanted this morning. Emma was not unattractive; her full, dark brows and green eyes made her stand out next to the usual mass of platinum blondes. The fullness of her brows revealed the gentle nature she was born with, which she was unable to conceal even in L.A. The uncontrollable head of curls contributed much to her daily chagrin; however, with that and a good portion of her stubbornness, she was able to survive this haughty city that was so infatuated by crime and vice.

Emma had to walk up and down the block on Figueroa Street twice before she found the store. Not that she hadn't expected something small, but this shop was nowhere to be found. When she walked up the 5700 block again, she looked closer in each shop window. There was one small boutique with food, Mexican clothing, and an undefined mix of toys and goods. It was a Mexican street market, stuffed into a one-woman shop. The chaos was enormous. Emma wondered how anyone could find anything in there at all. She passed one wedding gown shop, with dresses made from polyester for women who had to wed cheaply. Emma dreaded the outlook; one barber shop with self-satisfied Persians admiring their fresh, clean look in gold framed mirrors; and the next shop was empty.

Emma feared the worst. The typewriter shop had likely gone out of business. Had she driven all the way down here for absolutely nothing? Emma completely forgot about Aunt Nettie for a moment. Ray would be furious if his work was put on hold for another day just because he couldn't get his ink spool replaced. He was on summer break at Caltech, and this was the only time he had to continue his writing on *Thoughts*. She took one last glance at the end of the block. No one would assume a shop could be there, in a spot with barely two feet left on the side of the window front. Out of nowhere, the hidden entrance to a minuscule corner shop came into Emma's vision. Emma stopped and looked again, to verify that it was there. Its location was so unexpected, and its exterior odd and neglected. A filthy aluminum porte-à-faux covered the corner entrance. With a sigh of relief, Emma pushed the door open and smashed her curious nose against a wrought-iron security gate. *What on earth?*

"Good morning Mrs. Robinson!" smiled the shop owner from behind an old desk. The shop was small and stuffy, and every inch of space was cluttered with typewriter tools and parts.

He was a tall, grey-haired man wearing denim overalls. The years were painfully visible in his shop; the owner himself seemed to carry them away better. As so many Los Angelinos, he looked younger than he probably was. *That must be the sunshine*, Emma concluded. *It makes men look younger.*

"I have been expecting you," he added, and got up to open the gate.

Emma rubbed her nose. "I hope you didn't hurt yourself, Mrs....!"

"Miss Robinson," Emma interrupted.

"I see," the shop owner replied. "We are not married."

Quietly, she took in the dusty atmosphere of the antiquated world of the typewriter. "Astounding!" she said absent-mindedly.

"What is astounding, Mrs.—I mean, Miss Robinson?" The man asked.

"Oh! I'm sorry! I was just thinking out loud," Emma apologized. "I am impressed by your...patience, I guess. It must take many hours to repair machines like this, Mister..."

"Smith. My name is Raphael Smith."

She tried to be patient. Stores like these made Emma nervous: stores that dealt with equipment that was no longer available.

"Many hours, and a lot of skillfulness. Not a thing for impatient people, indeed."

"I see. I am here to replace my employer's ink spool."

Emma took a nervous glance at her gold Tissot wristwatch. It was ten past eight. That was okay. She wasn't sure it mattered what time she got back anyway, after what Ray had told her on the telephone.

"Nice watch!" Raphael noticed.

Emma quickly pulled her arm back. She knew that she shouldn't be wearing her gold watch in this neighborhood. She had inherited it from her father. She felt like she didn't remember him appropriately whenever she took the watch off, so she wound up leaving it on most days. Today would have been a better day to leave the watch at home. Definitely.

"The ink spool you wanted?"

"Yes, it's for a Persian..."

"I know." Raphael cut her off. "It's for a portable Persian typewriter. An Underwood. I remember that machine very well. He brought it in here a couple of years ago. It looked like it had traveled a long way. I had to realign all the letters. That was quite a job! I will never forget it. We had to take photographs of other Persian key tops to make sure we would place the letters correctly. His name is Randy or Ray...Winston, something like that. A teacher at Caltech."

"Ray West," it shot out of Emma. "Novelist and teacher."

"Of course. I should read more books."

"He's a really good writer," Emma insisted. "Not like many of these bestselling writers. His stories have *content*; he writes meaningful stories."

"Here is your ink spool, Miss Robinson."

It was fascinating, how little one end of the book had to do with the other. While the person typing their story on paper with a typewriter was probably dreaming of a better, more peaceful world with no gunfire, the one repairing the key tops was dreaming of just getting a few hours more sleep—dreading the wakeful customer who rung them out of bed early in the morning, like Emma. It was obviously time for Emma to leave.

"That will be fifteen dollars," Raphael said.

Emma handed him the cash. "Do you need a receipt?"

"Yes, Mr. Smith."

Quickly, he jotted a few words on a page in a notebook made specifically for that purpose, and tore it off.

"Here, Mrs. Robinson."

"Miss!"

"Of course, *Miss* Robinson. Have a good day."

"Good day to you, too, Mr. Smith."

Emma was already half out the door when the sun started to shine through. That was the one good thing about living in L.A. No matter how bad things got, the sun was almost always shining.

# Getting Arrested

The ride was easier on the way back to Pasadena. On the south side, the freeway was still congested. Everyone was headed downtown. Emma flew northbound against the stream—if such a thing was possible on the 110. It felt like the Monte Carlo Rally, with all the curves, bridges, and narrow entry ramps. Emma shook her head each time she read the speed limit that most people ignored on the off-ramps. It was 5 miles per hour, the speed of a bicycle rider on a holiday field trip. It was a miracle there weren't more accidents on this road.

As she continued to ponder the strange regulations of the Los Angeles traffic police, she thought back to how Aunt Nettie had acted at the movie theater last night.

"You should meet the new guy! He looks like James Bond, and is so friendly. I wonder why he doesn't have a girlfriend."

She had nothing but enthusiastic words about the new property manager. Despite all her efforts, Emma had only seen him very briefly in Ray's office, behind a half-closed door. Apparently the guy was very hard to locate. He appeared and disappeared randomly at odd hours. Maybe he was just very busy. Judging from what she'd heard about him, he must have been.

Natalie Woodbridge had been Emma's best friend since she'd moved into the backhouse at Ray's place, a few months ago. Emma didn't have many friends in L.A. It was easy to meet crazy people. However, to meet someone with a job and his own place, who wasn't crazy, was a challenge. Emma therefore stuck to Natalie Woodbridge. Aunt Nettie, as Emma called her lovingly, lived in the front house on the property next door. They went to see a movie every Sunday night.

The properties that Ray owned had originally been separate. However, when Natalie's husband passed away, Ray inherited his property under the condition that Natalie was to inhabit the front house for the rest of her life. They had remained childless, and except for some distant relatives, the Woodbridge's had no heirs. Natalie's husband had been a great fan of Ray's literature. Naturally, when it was time for him to write his last will, he left everything to Ray and his family. *What fans won't do for their idols*, Emma thought begrudgingly.

The backhouse on Natalie's side was rented to another childless couple, Alan Foster and Maureen Dorsay. The pair had been living there for twelve years. It had been Ray's wish not to change anything about the rental situation. He didn't have the time to deal with more work, so he hired a property manager to handle his rental business. That was the official version of the story, at least.

Emma always wondered why Ray didn't just let her handle the properties. Officially, it was because California laws required someone with a license to deal with property management. Practically, Emma couldn't figure it out. She had heard once, in a conversation between Ray and Katie, that the manager was related to Ray somehow. He was a cousin or a son from a previous marriage— Emma wasn't sure which. Ray rarely talked about his life before L.A. All she knew was that the new guy was *hot*, and she couldn't wait to catch a glimpse of his handsome face. He supposedly had the power to knock one out.

A maroon Infinity FX 35 SUV overtook her. The driver was invisible. *What kind of a person can stand sitting in a car like that?* She wondered. *It's preposterous!*

Her thoughts wandered back to the previous night. Her usually talkative Aunt Nettie, more so after the death of her husband, had been strangely silent. At first, Emma thought it might have been because of the movie she picked. It had been Aunt Nettie's turn to choose the movie, as they alternated each week, and she had decided she wanted to see *Life of Pi*. The movie had won an Oscar. Skeptic that she was, Nettie wanted to see for herself if it was worth the award. By the time they went to see it in the theater, it had already stopped running. Emma opted to watch *42*, the story of baseball legend Jackie Robinson. He was her namesake, after all. Emma had asked her many times if she was okay with the choice.

Each time, Nettie said, "Don't worry little angel, everything is fine."

*She called me little angel! Aunt Nettie was so nice.*

Then Emma thought she might not be feeling well. When Emma asked her about her health, Nettie shrugged her off and said, "Don't you worry about me, Emma, I'm fine. Just make sure you stay out of trouble!"

What awkward remarks Nettie was making! Emma couldn't make anything out of it. Her last recourse to making Aunt Nettie talk was the Persian guy—Aunt Nettie's favorite topic.

"What about the James Bond guy, have you seen him lately?" Emma remembered asking her.

Uncomfortable silence followed Emma's question. Nettie just stared at the big screen. Was it possible that Aunt Nettie was starting to develop a crush on the property manager, who was not even half her age? Emma had thought of her differently. However, you never knew. Old people were strange sometimes.

Emma took a glance at her Tissot. The clock on the dashboard was thirteen minutes off. It was 8:45 AM. Just enough time to get to Ray's house by nine: perfecto! Now that it probably didn't matter anyhow, she was going to make it there on time after all. The Toyota came to a halt at the stoplight where the freeway gives way to Arroyo Seco Parkway. She was now entering the city of Pasadena. Emma was relieved to be back where civilization had a small chance of survival. Being in Pasadena was not like being in Los Angeles, where humanity was forsaken entirely, suffocated by crime, vice, and corporate bureaucracy. Emma Robinson had grown a fatalistic worldview since moving to the City of Angels.

Filled with new hope after her exhausting excursion, she quietly let her not-so-new Toyota gently roll over the speed bumps on Wilson Street. It was only a 2007, but for L.A. standards, that was pretty old. People didn't get proper salaries here, but they all drove new cars. *Oops!* Emma failed to slow down enough for a bump. Her head smashed against the roof. *Darn it! Watch where you're going, girl,* she thought and rubbed her head. Emma missed the beat-up Oldsmobiles and squeaking Chevrolets she was used to seeing as a pedestrian in New York. Besides, back home she didn't need a car. She missed the good old days of not having to worry about bumps, scratches, and traffic tickets.

***

Kids were playing on the sunny playground at McDonald Park. Emma loved to watch the babies take their first steps on the sawdust surrounding the play area. Ray's house, a classic Craftsman with earthy green painted wood panels and a spacious porch in the front, was right across the street from the park. Natalie's home, a beige Craftsman with plaster walls and a brick chimney on the side, rested on the south lot. Similar to the backhouse on Ray's property, a concrete driveway led to Maureen Dorsay's house, which was quietly hiding in the back. A wooden fence defined the yard area that belonged to the front house, and a lock on the fence door kept the rear door of the house secured from intruders. Natalie, who hadn't experienced a single break-in in the entire thirty-nine years she lived there, usually left the rear door open for cross ventilation.

It was true, what Ray had said. A "whole arsenal" of police cars was parked in front of his house. Natalie's front door was open, and an ambulance was idling in front of it. *Oh my God,* Emma worried. She immediately recalled how strange Aunt Nettie had acted the night before.

Maybe her uncharacteristic silence was due to a feeling of nausea, a symptom that often precedes a heart attack. Maybe Aunt Nettie just kept quiet because she didn't want to upset Emma. *Oh Natalie, you should have said something! I would have called an ambulance for you right away.*

A police car blocked the driveway to the backhouse where Emma lived. Emma made a U-turn and parked on the street in front of the Chen's house, one lot north of Ray's. She jumped out of the car and rushed toward the ambulance, but her coat got stuck in the car door. By the time Emma freed herself, a friendly police officer with strawberry blonde hair and mustache had approached to help her. There was some gray mixed in his receding hairline. The roundness of his abdomen was telling of many tiring hours the man must have spent sitting at a desk. He might have been in his early fifties, and was not altogether bad looking. A younger, brown-haired, definitely very attractive lieutenant with an upper body that would make any woman's knees melt followed him. The lieutenant spoke with a slight accent that Emma thought was Greek, but she wasn't sure. A pair of pilot's sunglasses concealed his eyes. She wondered what his face looked like without those shades covering it all up.

"Give us a moment, Lieutenant," the detective said.

Emma read the lieutenant's nametag as he turned to walk in the other direction: Lieutenant George Savalas. *Bingo!* Her assumption of Greek family origin was confirmed. *If only I could catch a glimpse of his eyes*, Emma thought as she watched the sexy lieutenant walk away.

"Emma Robinson?" the detective continued toward her with authority. Emma turned toward the strong voice, irritated.

"I'm Detective Peter McGinnis, and I am the lead investigator of the Pasadena Homicide Division. Please follow me." Emma froze.

"Homicide?" she whispered.

"What happened to Mrs. Woodbridge?" she asked with a shaky voice as McGinnis escorted her toward the crime scene.

Now that Emma was paying attention, she was able to see that the porch area in Natalie's house had been roped off. Emma was starting to feel increasingly anxious. A chalk drawing traced the figure of a body lying on the floor between the doorway and foyer. Emma peeked around the doorframe and saw how a puddle of blood had stained Natalie's brand new beige carpet. McGinnis pulled her away to spare her the horrific image. Emma peeked at the crime scene anyway. A cold shiver ran through her body as she quietly took in what she could see of the gruesome scene. Finally, she tore herself away. Silent tears rolled down her cheeks.

"Aunt Nettie..." she whispered, but her voice failed her.

"I assume you were acquainted with Natalie Woodbridge, Miss Robinson?" The detective approached from a gentler angle.

"Yes, Sir," Emma answered. Telling herself to be brave, she wiped her tears away. "But will you finally tell me what happened here?"

"Well, we're still in the process of finding out ourselves. We are currently gathering evidence, so please don't access any of the concealed areas. What is certain is that Mrs. Woodbridge was murdered last night. Forensics estimates it happened somewhere between eleven PM and one AM."

Emma took a deep breath. That's exactly the time she remembered returning from the theater with Aunt Nettie. Ever since she had inherited that Tissot, Emma kept track of time almost meticulously. It was eleven PM when she said goodbye to Nettie at the doorway. *Oh my! Had I only waited for her to enter the house, maybe I could have saved her life!*

"It looks like somebody rang the bell, then entered the house and hit her over the head with a heavy object. She's fortunate in the sense that death was most likely instantaneous. It was a strong blow. We're still in the process of looking for the murder weapon."

"Oh, Aunt Nettie!" Emma cried aloud. The brutality of the event was too overwhelming for Emma. McGinnis had pity on her and handed over a handkerchief.

"Here, Miss." Emma wiped her nose.

"What was the exact nature of your relationship with Mrs. Woodbridge, Miss Robinson?"

Emma shook her head. These people from the police were terrible. She just wanted to be left alone.

"I'm her friend, Mr. Ginnis. Her neighbor."

"McGinnis, my dear," corrected the detective self-consciously. He was very proud of his name—but more than that, he was proud of his Irish heritage. He celebrated it on Saint Patrick's Day at the Lucky Baldwin's on Colorado Boulevard. That was the only day of the year that McGinnis went out to celebrate. He otherwise had no time for that. There were too many cases to solve in Pasadena.

"I met her at the Lake Street Café a couple of months ago. It was the first few weeks after I started," Emma explained.

"You work for Mr. West. Is that correct, Miss Robinson?"

"Yes, Sir. I am his editor."

"What were you doing last night between ten PM and two AM, Miss Robinson?"

"We went to the movies," Emma answered bluntly.

"Who is we?" the detective asked.

"Me and Aunt Nettie, why?"

"Oh no, not again," the detective remarked awkwardly.

***

Lieutenant Savalas returned to the crime scene. He cleared his throat. "Detective, I ah, can I speak to you for a moment?" He pulled the detective aside and pointed toward Emma's yard. Emma just stood there, dumbfounded.

"We found evidence," Lieutenant Savalas whispered. "It's in the young lady's yard."

"What kind of evidence?" the detective asked.

"Probably the murder weapon. It's a candlestick holder with trails of blood on it. One of those Jewish ones with seven arms," Lieutenant Savalas whispered.

"It's called a menorah, Savalas. And it seems somebody's trying to make that cute blonde over there look very bad," concluded the detective.

"I just wonder why," McGinnis said, and looked at her pityingly.

"What do you mean, McGinnis? You think we got another blonde case here?" asked Savalas, more for routine purposes than anything else.

"I sure think so, Savalas. Still, a living blonde is better than a dead blonde. Frankly, I'm glad that it was the old lady who got hit and not the young one, if you understand what I mean."

"I understand, Detective McGinnis—sort of."

Lieutenant Savalas took a step away. Jeez, sometimes he wondered why he didn't get a better job.

McGinnis was a good cop; there was absolutely no doubt about it.

In fact, Savalas was lucky to have found him here at the scene, and not some other big shot from homicide. At least McGinnis kept the politics out of the job, unlike many of the other officers.

McGinnis' contorted views about the blondes, on the other hand, gave him a stomachache. It must have been when McGinnis lost his wife to a young, alcoholic fashion model that he lost his sense of alignment. She had divorced him for a good-looking younger guy who had lost control of the car when he was drunk, driving her into thecement wall of a CVS Pharmacy. Alfio survived, but McGinnis's wife Lauren broke her neck. She was dead instantly. Savalas often thought Alfio would have been better off dead. Instead, he had to walk around with all that guilt on his conscience. Savalas almost felt sorry for him.

Heartbroken by the tragedy, Detective McGinnis walked away from the ordeal with a sense of entitlement and self-righteousness that was sickening.

"She should have stayed married to me, and everything would have been fine. Stupid blonde."

McGinnis' only defense for coping with the overwhelming sadness was sexism which Lieutenant Savalas, a happy soul, was forced to deal with since he was supposed to get along with the detective. He tried, but it was not always easy. Today, it was far from it.

As if there were a curse on their cases, their main suspect was a blonde woman—again. Not unattractive and apparently single, Savalas noticed, with a glance at her ring-less hand. Lieutenant Savalas decided that even if he couldn't save her from McGinnis' sexism, he'd at least be able to keep her alive. She was way too nice to lose. However, he knew pretty girls were killed all the time in cases like these.

***

When Emma saw the detective come out of her yard followed by the lieutenant, she knew that she was in trouble.

Savalas stared at her while she wasn't paying attention. When she looked back, he quickly averted his attention. Emma knew exactly what Savalas' eyes, hidden behind the pilot glasses, focused on. They were looking at the new suspect of this murder case—her.

*Stupid police: they're chasing the wrong one!*

"Miss Robinson!" Emma was surprised to hear the lieutenant's voice. He spoke very softly.

"Unfortunately, we have to arrest you. We have reason to believe that you are a suspect in this case."

In disbelief, Emma stared at her reflection in the lieutenant's sunglasses. How she hated those shades!

"On what grounds?" Emma asked with a shaky voice, in a last attempt to defend herself.

"I am sorry to inform you that the murder weapon was found in your back yard. Taking into consideration that you were the last known person Mrs. Woodbridge saw the night she died and that there was a piece of blonde hair next to the body, it looks like we have to take you with us. Even if it's just temporary," Savalas said, not without disappointment.

"A piece of hair?" Emma shot at him in disbelief.

"Yes, Miss. A blonde hair. It was a discolored or highlighted hair," Savalas explained in a matter of fact kind of way, looking closely at Emma's hairdo that had fallen apart. Affectionately, he took a wisp and tucked it behind her ear. He didn't show her the strand that he had picked off her blouse for evidence. He hid that in his palm for later.

Emma almost jumped. A highlighted blonde piece of hair next to Natalie's dead body. Of *course* she could have lost some strands of hair in Natalie's house; they were friends! What was this, circumstantial evidence only?

"You have the right to remain silent...," Savalas said mercilessly. Unable to control herself any further, she started to sob aloud.

Surprisingly, the lieutenant took off his sunglasses and put an arm around her shoulders. The Greek cop was apparently not only handsome, but kind as well. It turned out he had eyebrows. Emma was an old romantic. She liked strong men with full brows.

He gently escorted her to the police car, which he'd parked in her driveway. He was just about to open the rear door when the detective came around and held it open for her.

"Another tissue, Miss Robinson?" Savalas took his arm off her shoulder and let the detective take over.

McGinnis was still standing there, holding the car door in one hand and the tissue extended in the other. Emotionally destroyed, Emma grabbed the tissue and slid into the backseat of the police car. Only after she sat down did Lieutenant Savalas drop her hair strand into a plastic bag made specifically for collecting evidence. Before she could see what he was doing, he put the baggie into his shirt pocket, and then followed her into the backseat. McGinnis closed the door.

***

*Where has Ray been all this time?* If he had been there, he certainly would have helped her. If she had one thing in common with Ray West, it was a mutual disdain for L.A. police. Well, for the police in general, in Ray's case. Emma had once concluded that nobody comes out of a totalitarian country being fond of the police. She knew the police force wasn't *all* bad. Ray must be in at least as much trouble as she was. She was sure of it.

Also, a strange feeling of warmth arose in her bewildered heart as the handsome lieutenant helped her into her seat belt. *What are you thinking?!* Emma scolded herself. *This guy is a cop and he just arrested you. You should be turning into an ice cube.*

# In the Car

"Don't worry, Miss Robinson. You'll probably be released before the night is over. At the latest in twenty-four hours, when forensics brings the DNA test back. I would let you go right away, but seeing the evidence against you, we have to wait for that DNA result. After all, your hair does look fairly blonde to me," McGinnis spoke to Emma through the rearview mirror. She remembered speaking to her father in a similar way as she rode in the car, when she was still a little kid. Embarrassed, Lieutenant Savalas looked out the window.

The eye contact from her father had given her a sense of reassurance that children need when trapped for a long car ride. Coming from McGinnis, it felt like a threat. *Twenty-four hours locked in a holding cell based on the fact that I'm blonde! What a bunch of nonsense.* If her father was still alive, she would only need to make one phone call; he would bail her out right away.

Unfortunately, Emma got into trouble just a few months too late. Now her dad was dead, and her mom would never do such a thing for her. She wouldn't even know how. She was a linguist who suffered from so-called letter blindness. Other than her own high-end research, Dr. Hanna Behrend could not be relied on for a single thing. Her father had been the anchor that gave Emma a solid connection to reality. Emma's mother was a brilliant academic who crashed to the hard, unforgiving ground of reality as soon as the door to the university shut.

Feeling spiteful, Emma looked back into the mirror at McGinnis and said, "And what makes you so sure I didn't do it? After all, I am blonde!"

Nervous, Lieutenant Savalas curled his hands into fists and shook his head. *What is she doing? Is this woman insane?* He wanted to help her. With that attitude, however, he wasn't sure he was going to be able to do anything for her.

Detective McGinnis noticed the change. This time, he gave Savalas the well-meant fatherly glance through the rearview mirror.

"What's the matter, Savalas? Something not agree with you?"

"I'm fine, McGinnis. Just a little tired of being in a brunette minority here." The remark was just enough to change the detective's mood. He gave a loud, self-satisfied burst of laughter that resembled the chuckling tear of a lawn mower.

"You shouldn't take the detective so seriously, Miss Robinson," Savalas finally began. "He's a bit overly sensitive when it comes to troubled women, ever since he lost his wife in a car accident. She was a blonde, and according to McGinnis, if she'd had a different hair color, she would still be alive."

McGinnis' mood dropped instantly. "Ex-wife."

"Ex-wife. Sorry, McGinnis. Anyways, as I was saying, McGinnis has grown a little bit sensitive to the matter. An exaggerated sense of protectiveness overcomes him when he sees blondes. You shouldn't take it personally. He's a good guy."

"I'm not a troubled woman, Lieutenant Savalas. I happen to be very well. And I would appreciate it if you would refrain from any further sexist remarks regarding my gender and my hair color. Otherwise, I might have to open up a lawsuit against you for disrespectful demeanor while keeping me in custody. I doubt that would look good on your novice record."

"Of course, Miss Robinson. I will treat you with all due respect," Savalas complied. He wanted to punch himself for letting McGinnis' issues become his own. However, as long as McGinnis was the detective in charge, Savalas did not have much of a choice.

***

In a routine movement, McGinnis steered the police cruiser onto Garfield Street. Emma took in the beauty of City Hall's historic cupola in the distance. The austere façade of the courthouse and the historic Spanish buildings of the police department came into view. What normally filled her with a warming sense of hope for humanity left her numb today. It was suddenly all meaningless to her. *They are driving me to jail, while the murderer who brutally killed my best friend, is free to walk the streets.* Again and again, she concluded that the police just did not know what they were doing.

Emma's mood took another drop when McGinnis steered the car over to Ramona Street. They headed toward the courtside entrance of what was obviously the ice-cold façade of the four-story jail building. This L-shaped building, together with the older historic building of the police station, created an interior courtyard used as a parking area for police cars and jail buses.

"Welcome home," McGinnis said, more or less into the great void, as he pulled the key out of the starter.

Home? It was very clear that Emma's ideas of being home were quite different. McGinnis stepped out of the car, then waited for Savalas to step up to the other side of the car door. They would escort Emma to jail together.

McGinnis' remarks, which he probably thought of as witty, were getting to her. Working over twenty years in homicide would leave anyone disturbed. Especially having experienced a loss like McGinnis had. He was in denial over his broken heart, but projected it on others in a distorted kind of chauvinism. He protected women in front of the law, yet belittled them in his mind. Except Nell, of course; she enjoyed special status. Then again, Emma knew nothing about her, *yet*.

Emma was truly hoping this whole farce was going to be over withsoon. Spending only twelve hours in this hideous place was a prospect she could barely cope with. She couldn't help but hope for a miracle.

"May I?" Lieutenant Savalas extended his elbow in a sympathetic attempt to help her out of the car. Annoyed that her wish seemed to have come true in an unexpected way, she rudely brushed him off and got out by herself.

"I am sorry, Miss Robinson, I was just trying to be nice. But it looks like you are leaving me no choice but to apply routine procedures," Savalas said as he started to organize her soft hands behind her back and carefully placed a pair of ice-cold handcuffs on her wrists. In utter disbelief that this was happening to her, Emma stared into the void, devastated. McGinnis took one look at her face and knew what was going on.

"Trust me, Miss Robinson, by 8:00 AM we will have you out of here. That should be when forensics will be ready to present their reports. I'm sure we will also find more evidence on the murder weapon."

Emma did not trust a cop in L.A. at one mile of distance. She, herself, had gone on the streets many times in protest against the government. Why should she trust McGinnis?

McGinnis dismissed Savalas for the night and took over. He escorted Emma to the prison door. She secretly wished that Savalas were with her now. McGinnis was all she had at this point.

He punched in a code, and an automatic door slid open. "All doors are secured here; an escape is practically impossible. For a prisoner to get to the interior courtyard, he or she would have to pass three doors."

Emma did not care about the prison's security system. She was neither planning an escape nor planning to stay. Although how she was going to get out of this was a mystery to her.

An officer received them behind a glassed reception area. "Checking in, Ramalhes." Officer Ramalhes was a very proper looking middle-aged man. There was nothing special about him, nor was there anything wrong with him. Yet something about him bothered Emma. His brown–turned-gray hair was neatly cut, with a part on the left side. *Too neat*, Emma thought, as she studied the modest bureaucrat. *Too neat and too straight.* That was what bothered her. She was starting to feel claustrophobic.

Ramalhes gave her a routine face check. He seemed to hesitate for a fraction of a second when he hit her trusting eyes, of course. How could anyone send an honest citizen like her to jail? Mistakes with arrests did not often happen in Pasadena. There were far too many criminals running free in this town, and they were usually not so hard to catch. Nevertheless, arresting her was definitely a mistake.

***

Emma was terrified to meet her cellmates. She tried to hide it. First, she needed to have her mug shot taken. Ramalhes took care of her fingerprints right away.

"From this point on, Officer Hernandez will assist you," McGinnis explained as a female officer with straight brown hair held in a ponytail came out of the office area. She had even features and made a point out of her pretty face with a good application of makeup, just enough blush and light blue eye shadow over her brown eyes.

"This is Miss Robinson, Gina. She needs to be held until forensics brings us more results. You see, Miss Robinson was friends with the victim. They found a blond hair next to the body, as well as the murder weapon in Miss

Robinson's yard. I don't expect to keep her here for more than twelve hours, but procedure is procedure."

"I see. I am happy to hear that. Let me take your photograph and walk you to your cell, Miss Robinson."

Surprise overtook Emma. She felt almost a little sad that McGinnis was leaving now. Strange, how we can become attached to the people we resent. Apparently any human, no matter how annoying, becomes a comfort when the other is in crisis.

"I'll be gone for the night, Miss Robinson, but I will check on you first thing in the morning. Have a good evening!" McGinnis lifted his newsboy hat and left.

Emma thought she had not heard right: "Good evening?" How in the world could anyone wish her a 'good evening' when they were about to lock her up behind bars? This detective was clearly an awkward specimen of a man, Emma thought as she waved goodbye. Then her thoughts shifted to the Greek lieutenant. Boy, was she having a hard time not getting a crush on *that* guy. Even though she was feeling down in the dumps, a faint smile fluttered across her face.

But the moment her mood cheered up, Officer Gina Hernandez escorted her into the back office and took all her belongings from her: keys, her handbag with the typewriter ribbon, and the Tissot. Having to take off her watch, the one object that connected her to her father, was extraordinarily difficult. Emma did not want to give it up; Hernandez almost had to wrestle it away from her. "It belonged to my father," Emma explained.

"I understand, Miss Robinson, but you have to take it off for the time that you stay here."

Reminded again of where she was, Emma's courage fell into the cellar. Lacking any resistance, she let the woman take her watch. *What a tough person she must be, to have a job like this.* Emma was so grateful for her assistant's job, which after this disaster, she might never be able to practice again.

Officer Hernandez took her by the arm and led her to the corner of the room where the photos were taken. Emma had to stand in front of a white screen as Hernandez quickly operated the camera. Emma didn't smile; she couldn't. Even if she wanted to, smiling on official photos was forbidden, because it could affect the identification process in a negative way. Besides, her mood was too dark.

All Emma hoped for right now was that the other inmates would not be awful. She needed some distance from this horrific day.

"Follow me, Miss Robinson," Officer Hernandez said, as she fastened the cuffs on Emma's wrists.

# Ray's Alibi

Ray stepped out of the house. He was followed by Chief of Police Barthold Meane, from the homicide department. Bartholdo, as McGinnis had nicknamed him, was a step above McGinnis in the departmental hierarchy, and he let everyone know it.

Sometimes McGinnis wondered if Bartholdo wasn't just with the police making up for a lost career in academics. Bartholdo was rarely seen without a book dangling from his hands. Whatever his motivations were, McGinnis just hoped that Bartholdo's aspirations wouldn't culminate in a stint on the city council, as so many chiefs had attempted before him. In his more than twenty-five year long career at the Pasadena Police, McGinnis had seen it happen many a time: a good cop would go bad simply because they were starting to get ambitious in the wrong way. McGinnis preferred to remain unambitious and focus on his job, which was to solve crimes. Sometimes, though, he wondered why he didn't just make himself an independent. He knew there was enough crime out there for him to make a living from it. But the regular paycheck he was getting was just too comfortable right now.

At the police department, Bartholdo was mainly preoccupied with public relations. Normally he did not show up at crime scenes. When he heard that a murder had happened on Ray West's property, he decided to conduct the interview himself; if there was anything interesting about Bartholdo besides for his straight, lean,so very German appearance, it was his addiction to literature.

Whether or not the books that he read were of any value, McGinnis couldn't tell. He wasn't that much into literature. All he knew was that Bartholdo had no clue how to conduct a criminal investigation. That was frustrating for McGinnis because whenever Bartholdo took over a case, it almost guaranteed failure.

McGinnis was going to have to start the whole interrogation over from scratch as soon as he could, but not now. At the moment, it was Bartholdo's turn to stir up some useless dust.

***

Meane did not trust Persians. As the heir of Natalie's property, there were strong grounds to believe that Ray had a motive: he could finally tear some profit out of the whole situation and rent the house, once Natalie Woodbridge was done and dealt with. That's how Meane saw it, at least. It was an easy thing for Ray to blame the cute blonde from the backhouse. Just throw the weapon in her yard and place a hair on the crime site. Who knows where he found a piece of Emma's hair, but then again, that's what McGinnis was there for—to figure out all the annoying details.

Therefore, before he had to release him, he asked Ray about his alibi. He treated Ray West like any person, on purpose not granting him the respect a conversation with such a highly acclaimed writer might have called for. Ray wondered if the chief was jealous of his achievements.

"I was at the movie theater, Chief. I have about sixty-five witnesses," Ray said. He was a wise man. He was familiar with the methods of police power. Ray avoided using Bartholdo's name. That would prevent him from taking the whole thing any more personally than necessary.

"Name of the theater?" Meane pulled out an unused notebook. It was obvious that he had not a lot of experience conducting interrogations, which he hid behind an overly authoritative façade. His pen had dried out. Ray suppressed a laugh. He was a writer; he had pens everywhere. Ray walked to his desk and offered Bartholdo a Montblanc. Katie had given it to him for his fiftieth birthday, in 2008.

"This one works." Annoyed, the Chief of Police took the pen that his suspect handed him. He repeated the question in a most unfriendly tone. "Name of the theater?"

"Laemmle, in Santa Monica." If this hadn't been about his liberty, Ray would have cracked up laughing. *What an idiot!* Then again, they all were like that, at least most of them were. That's why they were in positions of authority; they *needed* them. Otherwise, no one would ever take them seriously.

Ray continued. "An independent version of my book is playing there, and the director asked me to be present at the evening showings. I am there every night, and I'm afraid I had nothing at all to do with my neighbor's killing. On the contrary, I very much wish she was still alive. Mrs. Woodbridge was a very sweet lady."

"But your first wife was killed in a Jewish bombing in Lebanon!" insisted Meane almost childishly. "You have an anti-Semitic motive!" He had done some research on Ray's family history and found out that Ray had lost his first wife, Hafa, in the shelling of Kana on April 18, 1996. She had been volunteering as a nurse on the United Nations compound. They'd had a child together.

"That was almost twenty years ago, Mr. Meane. And contrary to what you might think, I am not an anti-Semitist. If you were in any ways familiar with the deeper content of my work and not just with the bestseller, you would understand that I am a pacifist by conviction, and I would never discriminate against anyone for their religious views, be it a Jew, an Islamist, or anyone else. How else do you think I can stand being married to a Jewish woman? Please excuse me now, Mr. Meane. I believe you have my alibi to check, and I have work to do."

Ray West led Meane off the porch. Meane had never made it beyond the entrance hall. It took some talent to get access to a suspect's house when you weren't holding a warrant in your hand, which Meane did not possess at this point.

Furious, Ray West suddenly made an 180-degree rotation and strode toward Meane. "The pen, please!" Ray reminded him. "It's a present from my wife. I would hate to lose it."

Without a word, Barthold Meane handed him the pen.

No matter how many books he read, Meane knew that McGinnis was usually one step ahead of him. Just like this entirely uneducated individual, McGinnis was able to analyze the move of a world-class chess player without any background in chess, if he had to. Meane did not know how he did it. That's why, deep inside, he knew he needed McGinnis. That didn't necessarily make things any better.

Still, Meane felt that Ray was obviously withholding something. So much so that he, Barthold Meane, could tell, from the many passive years of criminal investigation that he had practiced. He didn't know what, though. He would have to send McGinnis out to uncover the truth about Ray West's secrets. Again, this made him resent McGinnis just a little more.

# Locked Up

Another sliding door opened into the barred area of the recently admitted inmates, as Officer Gina Hernandez explained the number of women there. "About ninety percent of the women here were caught driving under the influence. A lot of them are just sobering up right now."

Emma took in the stale smell of transpired booze evaporating from the women's bodies, mixed with the smell of perspiration. It was nauseating. She tried to distract herself from the bad air by getting into prison statistics—the last topic she'd ever thought she would be entertaining any thoughts about. "And who are the other ten percent?" Officer Gina was fumbling with what resembled a credit card. It was her all-access key to the cells. The days when they used actual metal keys for the cells were long gone in the city of Pasadena.

"Thieves, burglars, prostitutes, and homicide suspects, Miss Robinson. We keep actual murderers in separate isolation cells in the south block. As long as they are only suspects, they get to share cells with all the other women. If no proof of their innocence can be found and they are scheduled for a court trial, the murder suspects get transferred into isolation cells, which are located in the south wing."

Officer Hernandez thought that Emma needed to hear the exact fate of the homicide suspects located in the Pasadena jail. She did not know that was the last thing Emma would want to know. All that Emma wanted was to get out of there.

When Officer Gina halted in front of cell number 107, where Emma was going to spend the night, her mood arrived at ground zero. Only pride withheld her tears.

In front of Emma, the scarce universe of a prison environment opened up. Emma looked at two bunk beds, placed on each side of the wall; one other female was already in the cell. She sat with crossed legs on top of the bunk on the left, and her thick, brown, curly hair hung in a wild bush over her brownish face. Emma noticed that the woman had freckles. She was one of these women whose fate was to be blessed with beauty, no matter what else happened to them. Emma admired her stunning face for a moment—then the truth of this woman's reality kicked in.

Still, Emma sighed with relief. At least she wasn't going to be attacked by a gang of crazy women. There was only one other woman. Maybe they would get along. Officer Gina slid her card through the reader, and the bars opened. "This is your cell. The other inmate's name is Adriana Cunningham. Have a good night, Miss Robinson."

"What's the new inmate here for, Officer Hernandez?" A shy, but scratchy voice quivered from the top of the bunk bed.

"Miss Robinson is a homicide suspect," Officer Hernandez answered shortly, while she opened Emma's handcuffs. Emma heard a long silence that under normal circumstances should have been a 'pleased to meet you.' Emma must have scared the woman to death. This was horrible! She had to convince her that she had nothing to fear of her.

"And don't you get into each other's hair, ladies. There is nothing more stupid than getting jail time while otherwise you could have been free. I've seen it happen a thousand times; women who were going to be released wound up spending months in jail, just because of some stupid difference of opinion. Trust me, ladies; I know what I am saying. It's better to get along."

Adriana and Emma stared at each other. Neither had any intention of getting into any type of brawl. They both just wanted to get out, and as fast as possible.

"Good night, now," Officer Hernandez said as she slid her card again, which activated the bars to close. After she had made sure that the bars were all locked and safe, she started to walk back to the office. The hollow clacking of the officer's shoes echoed through the entire hallway, from the cell to the sliding door, until she was gone. The women were so quiet she could hear them breathe, Emma noticed with utter discomfort, for she couldn't see their faces. Emma hadn't moved an inch since Officer Hernandez had taken off her cuffs. She just stood there and listened to the officer promenade across the prison hallway until the sliding door swallowed her sound. That it was a promenade was undeniable. This was a walk of power through the anxious inmates, waiting for news from their only messenger of the outside world: the prison officer.

***

McGinnis wanted a beer. He needed something to wind down from this crazy day, so he could plan what to do tomorrow. He usually did this before he left his office on Garfield Street at headquarters, but today had been exceptional. He had to leave the premises of the police station to gain some distance. After all, it wasn't every day that he locked a young blonde away.

He usually found them dead, and had to resolve the question of what had gotten them there. Now, he needed to resolve what got this one into jail, and it was certainly not a homicide—not one that *she* had committed, anyway.

"'Anything new, Detective?" Tim Simmons was an upbeat, brown haired, tall, and handsome Australian student at PCC who worked at the Irish bar to help pay for his classes in criminology. He had taken an immediate liking to the detective when he had first served him.

"Not really. Only this blonde from New York, who went to jail for the night."

"A DUI?"

"Am I with the traffic police?" Simmons just shrugged in reply.

"No. She's a homicide suspect," McGinnis explained.

"Homicide, wow! So you're on another blonde case. Let me get your drink. Same as usual?"

"Same thing. I just can't seem to get around them blondes anymore," the detective sighed.

Tim Simmons was already off to the bar. They always had around a half a dozen glasses of Guinness prepared on the counter at night. It was the most popular drink at the pub, and it took around five minutes for the foam to settle: too long for customers to wait. Tim picked up a glass and dashed back to the detective's booth, way in the back. When McGinnis came to the pub, he wanted to be left alone. Sitting near the entrance was usually a bad idea, because that was the area where most fights happened. As an officer off duty, if a fight started, it was still his job to intervene until the appropriate patrol car had arrived. When he was sitting in the back of the room with his back to the entrance, he followed a different policy: "What I don't see does not concern me, and I leave it up to the club patrons to handle the situation."

Tim put down the glass and took a seat opposite McGinnis in the booth. It was Monday night, and the bar was not too crowded. "So tell me!"

McGinnis took a sip and leaned back. He was finally able to relax. Tim was a good dude. It didn't bother him that Tim asked holes into his stomach. Reviewing his cases with Tim usually made him see a point that he had overlooked in the course of the day.

"Well, this Jewish woman got hit over the head with a menorah, and somebody is trying to make it look like the writer's assistant did it."

"What writer?"

"Ray West."

"Oh, I know: *Flames of Passion*. I read the book. The guy was all over the news for a while, when he won the Nobel Prize in 2006."

"And?"

Tim just looked at the detective, confused.

"How is the book? Do you recommend it?"

"Oh, you mean was the book any good! *Of course* it was good. A little bit too much on the tacky side for my taste, but even seeing all the violence in the world now and all that's going on in the precarious Middle East, I have to admit it still felt very revealing in the end. I'm just not the romantic type, Detective. I read the book because I wanted to see what a story reads like that won the most prestigious prize in the world!"

Detective McGinnis felt Tim's comments somewhat confirmed the idea he had about Ray West's book. An audience hit that was overrated because it had a romantic ending—and that played in an area where people are normally used to experiencing tragedies. It was not the first time that a mediocre piece of writing had gotten an award just because its writer had a good sense of current fashions. It was not going to be the last. *Ray West must be a smart guy, to place his story in the area that the whole world is looking at right now: The Middle East.* McGinnis made a mental note to ask West about his views on the conflict and took another gulp.

"I see. So I don't need to read the book. That's good. I don't have any time for that kind of trivial stuff, anyhow."

Tim burst into a fit of laughter. "Trivial literature! The book won the Nobel Prize in Literature, the most prestigious award a writer can get, and he's been on the top of the bestseller list for months!"

"Still, according to you, there's nothing unexpected in the plot, is there? Just another romance in an area of conflict, right?"

"Yes, that's true, Detective."

"So I don't need to read the book."

"Maybe not. But I have another question. Who is this assistant who works for West? I wouldn't mind having a job like that. Instead, I have to work my butt off in a dump like this!"

A soccer fan wearing a Tiburones Rojos de Veracruz outfit called for beer. "Hey, Camarero!"

Quickly, Tim Simmons went to the bar and gave the thirsty fellow his drink. Tim rushed back to the detective's booth because he couldn't wait to hear more about the case.

"She's a linguistics major from NYU, Tim. As innocent as an unprinted piece of paper, if you ask me."

"Why did you put her in jail, then?"

"There is some evidence against her. The murder weapon was found in her yard, and they found a blond hair near the body."

"Is she the only blonde that lives on the property?" Tim wanted to know before he got up to serve an African American girl with too high heels and her boyfriend, a huge Mexican with shoulders as broad as a closet.

*Of course!* In the turmoil over the famous writer, they had completely forgotten to check the people in the backhouse. He took out his phone and sent Savalas a text message:

Did anyone get any information about the people who live in the backhouse of the former Mr. Woodbridge's property?

McGinnis took a huge gulp from his glass that now was half-empty. The reply came back immediately.

"Checked the backhouse while you took care of the suspect. Apparently, a childless couple lives there. A Miss Maureen Dorsay and Alan Foster. They went to Arkansas for a week for the purpose of adopting a child."

The detective replied:

"Interesting! Does anyone have any information about the couple's hair colors?"

The answer came back quickly.

"I already got that: Mrs. Dorsay has bleached blonde hair, but since the couple was away for foster purposes, I don't assume that they are suspects."

*Aha. There it is. The missing detail.* McGinnis knew that he had forgotten something.

"Meet me at my office first thing tomorrow morning. We're doing another search!"

"Consider it done. See you tomorrow, Detective. Take it easy on that beer…"

"I don't need a nanny, Savalas; I can watch over myself. I just need a lieutenant who's there on time."

"No worries, McGinnis: punctuality is among my assets. I'm always on time."

*He can be really annoying sometimes,* Savalas thought, *especially when he's interrupted during happy hour.*

Tim came back. McGinnis took another long gulp and emptied the glass. "So what's next, Detective? Are you going to arrest the Persian writer instead?"

"I don't know yet. It's possible. All I know is that I definitely don't care about his book. Falling in love in a war zone is not like real life. At least, it's certainly not like *staying* together. In reality, couples get divorced over trivialities every day. If they don't get separated and think they're happy, one of the partners dies, probably either in a car accident or because of cancer. That's reality. I don't think I'm a big fan of fiction, Tim. And most definitely not one of Ray West's novels. Good night, now, and don't let any of your patrons get your good spirits down. You're a great guy, Tim Simmons."

"Of course not," Simmons smiled. It was true: if the sarcastic spirit of McGinnis couldn't get him down, nobody could. That was probably why he worked in a pub: he was one of the few who could handle it.

"Good night, Detective."

Detective McGinnis gave Tim Simmons a wave with his newsboy hat as he stepped out of the bar. Lucky as he was, he lived only a block away from the Irish Pub, on Michigan Street. In an instance of good foresight, he had parked his car in his garage in the apartment complex, walking to the bar. Even though he was a heavy guy, a Guinness was still a Guinness, and a DUI was the last thing the detective needed on his perfectly clean driving record.

# Adriana Cunningham

"Stop staring at me!" Adriana Cunningham finally shouted from her cross-legged position on her bunk bed. She spoke with a thick New York accent, mixed with some Latino. Emma still had not moved since she had first entered the cell, and her cellmate's beautiful face must have held her unconscious attention.

Emma suddenly woke up. The realization that she was in jail hit her like a sledgehammer. Finally, she sat down on the lower bed on the right side of the cell and started to cry.

Emma sobbed, sobbed, and sobbed some more, for ten minutes straight. She didn't know how long she had been sitting there, and she did not completely understand why. Partially, she was crying over the recent lossof her dad, whom she hadn't had enough time to mourn because she had moved to L.A. so quickly. It all came over her at once. The tears would not stop flowing.

"It's oookay! Stoooap crying!" the girl said, with her familiar accent. Each 'o' sounded very long, and she pulled them into an 'a' in the end. Emma immediately felt at home. How she missed that accent. She hadn't heard it in anyone since she had arrived in L.A.

Emma wiped her tears away. "I'm sorry." She chuckled a little. The absurdness of her situation made her laugh. She had been in Los Angeles for three months, and it took a night in jail for her to finally start talking to someone from her hometown.

"Stop apologizing! You're okay. I sat here for over an hour and cried my soul out when they brought me here. There was not a soul in this cell when I walked in here this morning. I'm Adriana."

The attractive young woman jumped down from her top bunk bed, walked across the prison cell to Emma's side, and gave her a hug. Emma was speechless. All she knew to do was to hug the friendly woman back. "I'm Emma Robinson." They held on for what seemed a lifetime; somebody had just made a new friend. Then Adriana eventually let go.

"You're not a murderer." She stared straight into Emma's face, then scrutinized her figure and outfit. "Murderers don't dress like...well, *you*!"

Emma chuckled a little, helplessly trying to stop her tears and her running nose. "Tissue?"

Adriana pulled a huge pile of toilet paper off the roll and quickly brought it to Emma. There was no real Kleenex in sight. That made Emma smile. She wiped the tears off her face and cleaned her nose.

"No, I'm not."

"That's what I thought the first minute I saw you. You're way too proper to be a murderer."

"Ah, ha-ha." That made Emma laugh. "Too proper. I'm all messed up!" And she glanced into a small wall mirror beside the bunk bed.

"What are you in here for?" Strands of hair had fallen out of her bun, and it was too messy, even for Emma's standards. She decided to open up the bun and reset her hair into a ponytail.

"Boy, you got a thick pile of hair on your head, girl. No one could tell, when it's all put up in a bun like that!" Adriana noticed.

"Not as thick as yours is."

"Ah, mine's a wild chaos!" Adriana said, revealing the amount of work it takes to take care of a head of corkscrew curls like that.

"A beautiful chaos!" Emma said. "Thank you."

"So what are you in here for?" Emma insisted.

"Ah, you don't wanna know."

"Yes, I do! After all, what are we going to talk about in here all night?"

Adriana sadly looked on the cold, gray, cement floor. "Domestic violence."

Emma was shocked. "What, you?"

Adriana looked at Emma and didn't know if she should laugh or cry. Emma was right. It was all wrong.

"Yes, honey. Domestic violence is a serious offense. You wouldn't give it to a tiny little woman like me with a healthy heart and soul to do a thing like that, yet it's true; I slapped my boyfriend in the face when he called me a worthless whore."

"Oh my goodness, what an insult! I would have slapped him, too." "Yes, honey, but in the state of California, hitting is considered an act of domestic violence. It doesn't matter how soft it was. You can hit your partner over the head with a box of tissues, and they will still put you in jail."

"Well, in my case, they are trying to tell me that I hit an old lady over the head with a menorah."

"Oh my goodness, that *is* serious!"

"Oh yes, it is. The worst thing is, she was my friend. That's why they brought me here. I am the last one to have seen her before she died."

"Oh my God, poor old lady. Who would kill an old lady? It must be someone with no heart or conscience: a terrible person, not you!"

"Yes, I know. The police think they'll get me out of here by tomorrow morning. They don't really believe I did it, either. Only, all the evidence was placed to make it look like I did it."

"Oh, my. You mind?" Adriana had to sit down on the lower bunk bed on Emma's side. This whole day was too overwhelming.

"And I thought that I was in trouble. Homicide suspect—that's huge! You got any clues who might have done it?"

Emma sat down beside her cellmate and started to use her investigator's brains. "Not really. On one hand, Ray West has motive. If Natalie dies, he can rent out the place and collect money for it. He was unable to do that because of a hidden clause Natalie's husband put in the contract. But Ray isn't a bad person. Clearly, he can be quite annoying at times. But he's not a murderer. No. It most certainly was not Ray."

"Who then?" Adriana rolled a curl around her index finger, pulled it straight, and let it pop up again.

"If I only knew. Aunt Nettie's husband is already dead, so there's no drama possible on that side." Emma tapped her fingers against her temples and thought.

"Maureen and Alan went out of town to visit the surrogate mom. So they couldn't have done it, even though Maureen is, frankly, bizarre."

"Terribly bizarre, or just odd bizarre?" Adriana helped, letting another curl pop.

"I don't know. I really don't know Maureen all that well. I've kind of kept to myself after I heard her argue with her husband so much."

"What were they arguing about?" Adriana stopped what she was doing and listened closely.

"I couldn't hear the details, because I was working in dictation with Ray. But when I got out for a moment to take a break, I heard Maureen say something about not wanting any children from Alan, and then she started saying something about drinking alcohol. I never heard the rest of the conversation, which was very loud, because Ray called me back into his office to do more dictation."

"So you think it was just a random act of violence?"

"What do you mean? Somebody just knocking at the door, Natalie opens, and they kill her?"

Adriana nodded. She was back to popping her curls.

"Not possible. If it was somebody from outside, they would have forced their way in, grabbed the menorah, and hit her then. One would think that Aunt Nettie would have either rushed back inside or ran away, but her body was lying right in the doorway. No, the killer must have been inside when she got back from the movies. It seems like he was standing in there waiting for her when I was on the porch, saying goodbye. He killed her as soon as I walked off the porch, before she could even close the door."

"Scary!" Adriana popped one last curl and got up. "I think I need to turn in. I'm tired of figuring things out."

Adriana got up and practically sleepwalked across the cell to her bunk bed.

"Wait a minute!" Emma exclaimed.

Adriana stopped and turned around. "Huh?"

"There *is* one thing that was very strange about Aunt Nettie last night.

"What was that?" Adriana was only listening with half an ear while she climbed up the ladder to the top bed.

"You see, there's this guy Ray hired to do the property management. Natalie talked about him all the time."

"Is he hot?" Adriana plopped into her bed and went back to sitting cross-legged, which seemed to be the position she was most comfortable in.

"Apparently, yes!"

"What do you mean, apparently? You don't know what your property manager looks like?"

"No, I don't! When I first arrived here, Ray handled everything. So I didn't have to deal with him. It was Aunt Nettie who was talking rivers about him, until last night. Then she was awkwardly silent. When I tried to cheer her up and asked about the property manager, she didn't respond. I thought she might have gone senile and developed a crush on him. But then she was found dead in her doorway!"

"Is he *that* hot?"

"I personally have never seen him up close. I put my rent check in the box each month and the next day, zap! It is gone. I have never heard anyone open the box, or seen someone walk to or away from the property. It's as though the guy was wearing an invisibility cloak. I do believe he drives a maroon Infinity SUV, though. I've seen that car parked in our lot. But the owner of the car has always mysteriously been missing, or locked in a conversation with Ray, where I was asked not to enter the room."

"Maybe *he*'s bad? Good looks don't mean anything!" Adriana knew. She was in the midst of her evening meditation, and listening only with half an ear.

Emma was meanwhile reliving her past three months of Los Angeles experience all over.

"I don't know him, so how can I tell?" Emma reflected. It was true.

She had only seen him one time, sitting in Ray's office. He had been using Ray's chair, and turning it in circles like a big shot. She remembered catching a glimpse of his brown hair, and the angle of his brows, which seemed too perfect to be true. He must have been as good looking as Natalie described him, which made him a suspect by the laws of nature. According to Emma's logic, anyone with very good looks was a potential danger to society. Yes, he might be a murderer, but he had no motive. Why would he want to kill an innocent old lady whom he had nothing to do with? It didn't make sense. There must be something she wasn't seeing.

"Why would the property manager want to kill the old lady? There's no benefit to that for him. No, it must be someone else."

"Ooooohmm." Adriana was doing her yogic ohms to terminate the meditation process.

"If you say so. I have to get some rest now. I have a tough day in court ahead of me tomorrow. I have to explain to them that I was acting in self-defense."

"Can you claim you were acting in self-defense when someone verbally insults you?" Adriana had torn Emma out of her traumatic flashback, back into jail reality.

"No. But Anthony has been beating me regularly for many years now, whenever he comes home drunk and doesn't find me at home waiting for him. I've never said anything because I thought I loved him. But maybe, now that I'm sitting in here instead of him, it might be my turning point."

Adriana lay down and pulled the blanket over her head. Disgusted, Emma forced herself to use the toilet and then she lay down, too.

"I'm all for it, Adriana. I hope you win. Abusive men should not have great women, as I'm sure you are. They don't deserve them. They should be shown otherwise."

"Ah, you darlin' sweetheart. I hope you do get out here by tomorrow, just like they promised you. Women like you don't belong here."

"Oh, thank you for saying that, Adriana. I hope you get out, too."Good night now," Adriana stared onto the ceiling when the night warden came out of the sliding door and made her routine patrol.

"Lights out, ladies! Bed rest!"

The jail had fallen silent again as soon as the sliding door opened. It had a magical effect on the inmates. It was as if the entire room was holding a collective breath. Emma barely dared to breathe. The sliding door closed. Exhale!

"Good night, Adriana," Emma whispered. "You're a good soul. You shouldn't be dealing with that kind of guy."

"I know, darlin'. Good night, now." Adriana sighed.

*I will! I will,* Emma decided firmly. *I won't let these stupid police people take away my integrity. I will take this case into my own hands if I have to, and show them who the real murderer is! Natalie deserves to have the truth found out.* Emma tried to remember the traits of the manager in more detail, and pondered. What if he *was* so good-looking that Natalie could have fallen for one so much younger than she was? However, Emma could barely remember what he looked like, much less make any sense of the possibility. So, frustrated, she sighed and went to sleep at last.

***

McGinnis was sitting more healthily than happily in his office chair, feeling like an egg that had just popped. He was experiencing the pseudo-euphoric feelings caused by the release of endorphins from the consumption of an unexpected amount of alcohol, and the beginnings of a slight hangover. Once the endorphins stopped spilling out, the headache would set in. McGinnis was not used to going out drinking anymore. Not even a single pint of Guinness! Well aware of what would come next, he opened the drawer to his desk and swallowed an aspirin. He could not afford to walk around with a headache. The case needed to be solved. Soon he would be back to his usual fake smile and foul mood.

McGinnis was usually grumpy in the morning. A therapist's analysis would have been "Chronic depression." However, his strong-willed personality did not allow for any feelings of sorrow, which in *his* worldview were an expression of weakness. McGinnis aspired to heroism like that of the heroes in the storybooks—and in the books, heroes never cried. Hence, he was grumpy.

While McGinnis reminisced about the bittersweet taste of the beer that had gone down his throat last night, Lieutenant Savalas suddenly stormed in through the half-open door.

"Your mother not teach you to knock when you walk into someone's office, Lieutenant? What's the big deal?"

"The suspect: she got out!"

McGinnis stayed perfectly calm. "Miss Robinson?"

"Yes, Detective. The writer guy paid her bail and got her out before daybreak."

True, McGinnis was slightly surprised to hear that Ray had bailed her out. Just slightly, for nothing truly surprised him anymore.

"Interesting," McGinnis stated. "I guess that spares me a walk through the depressing rooms of the Pasadena jail. I was going to check on her and give her a heads-up."

"Not necessary, Detective. Suspect cleared the rooms."

"Well, I guess that leaves me with no choice but to check West's alibi. It seems bulletproof."

"It is, Detective. I spoke to three parties who attended the Santa Monica screening. They all confirm that Ray was there all night."

"All night, so. Well, I'm not so sure about that. Any word from forensics?"

"Yes, Detective. The hair cannot be identified. The bleaching ruined the structure of the DNA, and so what's left for us as evidence is like a washed out piece of fabric: there's nothing on it. Also, if Emma really was Miss Woodbridge's friend, her hair might have been laying around there anyhow, so our evidence is not really all that significant at this point."

"Of course it isn't. You're confirming my assumption. The evidence that's found near the victim always serves to lead the investigation into the wrong direction. That's why the killer puts it there in the first place. No, no, no... We have to approach this case from an entirely different angle."

"Which would be?"

"As for my part, I am going to start with Mr. West's family history. You can tell me what you want, and you can name all the literary prizes in this world, something about this man is fishy. People who change their names always have something to hide. I don't care how famous they are. Ray West stinks. And I am going to find out what's causing the stench."

"His real name is Nadir Tabish Esfahani. It means 'The precious brilliant man from Teheran.'"

"All the more reason not to trust him, a man with a name like that: how pretentious!"

"You don't like him very much do you, Detective?"

"I'm a cop. My job is not to like or dislike people; my job is to find out the truth about them. Just between us, I'm not a poetic kind of guy. Literature is not my world. I guess that's the only thing I agree with old Bartholdo on—I do *not* trust Ray West."

"Maybe if you read one of his books, it would change your perspective. I started reading *Flames of Passion.* It's quite good!"

McGinnis was getting slightly annoyed.

"My job is not to change my perspective; it *is* to find a murderer. So, sorry, no time. Anything else, Savalas?"

Lieutenant Savalas, who was looking forward to his lecture of the book during his fifteen-minute break, couldn't remember.

"Not at the moment." He made his way back out of grumpy McGinnis's office, whom the morning was clearly too early for, still.

Savalas stopped in the doorframe.

"I checked the family in the old lady's backhouse. Alan Foster and Maureen Dorsay, a married couple, flew to Arkansas two days ago to meet the surrogate mother of their adoptive child. I believe I've told you this already. They couldn't have done it. They weren't even here."

"You're drawing premature conclusions, Lieutenant. You still have a lot to learn. Of course they could have done it."

"How? They weren't there!"

"With a menorah, remember?"

Lieutenant Savalas was confused. It was time for his fifteen-minute break. "I don't get it. Anything else, Detective?"

"I want you to check the airport, Savalas. Like with Ray at the movies, I need to know if they actually showed up in the airplane or if they just bought a ticket. Anyone can purchase a ticket these days, with the Internet and all. That doesn't mean that they actually *went* somewhere. Even *I* can figure *that* out. Notice, that's coming from a man who remembers when the electric typewriter was a huge technological invention!"

"Consider it done, Detective. Anything else?" "I want you to take her for lunch."

Savalas froze. "What: Who?"

"The girl. Emma," McGinnis answered, as if it was the most normal procedure in the world.

"But..."

"You never know what people know. Usually, they don't even know it themselves. She's definitely not our suspect, but what better way to get information about Ray, than to hear the person out who writes down all his thoughts? She might have picked something up that not even she is aware of. Make an excuse, and bring her some flowers or something. And no worries. She won't turn you down. You're too good-looking."

McGinnis was the one who had everything under control. That much was clear to Savalas, and he never attempted to have it any other way. However, today, Savalas definitely didn't have anything under control. It was time for his coffee break.

"Consider it done." Savalas quickly disappeared into the hallway.

"He has a bulletproof alibi, the old Iranian. How annoying! Let me see how good it really is," McGinnis thought aloud, which was an old habit of his. Hearing his own voice made him feel more important in his role as a homicide detective. After his ex-wife had died in the car accident, his job meant everything to him. Time and again, he couldn't emphasize enough the difference his persona made in the Pasadena Police Department. Of course, no one was aware of that. Except Nell, maybe.

# Back

Emma had a hard time keeping her eyes open as she sat in the passenger seat of Ray's 1958 green Bentley. It was six o'clock in the morning.

"But why did you come out here so early, Ray?" Emma wanted to know.

"The kids have to go to school. Katie leaves too early to drive them. Bringing Jasmine and Mike to school is my job, has been so since always."

"Does she know that you bailed me out?" Emma was quite over- whelmed by this unexpected act of generosity by her employer, who had given her so many reasons to resent her job in the past. He was changing her perspective drastically.

"She advised me to bail you out. She is an ace at setting priorities, and always has amazing advice. You see, Katie figured out that the sooner I get *Thoughts* out, the better for everyone. *Flames* will sell better, and I will make some money with *Thoughts*, as well as sending a positive message out to the world. So even though your bail was not cheap, it's cheaper for us to continue having you work on *Thoughts*, and it's better for the world, too."

*Wow!* Emma was overwhelmed. She was not used to dealing with such large sums of money, and a lot of what Ray was saying went in one ear and out the other. All that remained in her head was that her participation in the *Thoughts* project was somewhat important, and the fact that she desperately needed some sleep.

The rough wool blanket on her prison cot had left her freezing all night, along with the worries of the past day. She wondered how McGinnis was going to react when he heard that she'd been bailed out. *He'll probably freak out and start chasing after Ray because that's his only other suspect*, she concluded. She decided to protect Ray as much as he had protected her.

***

The green Bentley rolled smoothly into 987 Wilson Street. Katie, with her bulky red leather LV handbag and a blue dress suit that suited her curvy figure perfectly, was saying goodbye to her kids. They were standing in the hallway with their clothes half on their bodies and half scattered around them. "Daddy will do that!" Katie said. She was running late.

"Hi Daddy." Jasmine smiled.

"I'm going all in blue today, Dad," Mike said.

"Hi kids, I'll be there in a minute," Ray shouted through the open car window.

Even though taking care of the kids in the morning was Ray's job, Emma had the feeling that she was the one who'd get to finish dressing the kids today. There was too much chaos going on for Ray to handle it. Besides, she loved kids and felt obliged to do something for Katie, her generosity had been so overwhelming.

Ray turned the key, and the Bentley fell silent. Katie smiled at Ray when she saw him open the car door. Emma felt like she had entered an oasis of peace amid the mind-boggling turmoil of the past day. From now on, everything was going to be okay, Emma decided. All she needed to do was help McGinnis find the culprit, which most certainly was not Ray. As smart as McGinnis looked, Emma figured he was maybe not smart enough to solve this case. She definitely did not know him well.

Worried, Katie threw Emma a glance. "You look like you need some rest, honey," Katie shouted, digging deep into her handbag to find the car keys.

"Thank you so much for helping me, Katie. I will never forget this..." Katie finally found the keys. She yanked them out of the bag and held them up high against the sunlight to convince herself that they were really there. God knows what else was in that handbag.

"No big deal, Emma. You're a good girl. You shouldn't have had an experience like that because of us." Katie walked to her red Alfa Romeo sports sedan, parked in front of Ray's Bentley.

"You're going to have to move your car, Ray, if I'm ever gonna make it to work this morning."

"Sure, dear." Ray hopped back into the car and moved it onto the street while Emma walked up the steps to the porch, where the half- dressed boy was standing. Jasmine was standing there in a white dress with a delicate flower print.

"What a pretty dress you're wearing!"

"Thank you. Can you help Mike get dressed, please? He's all messy."

Mike was trying to get into his blue polo shirt, but couldn't get his arms threaded into the sleeves.

"Let me help you with that." Emma slipped the shirt on him and buttoned him up. "What a handsome boy you are!"

"I need this, too!" Mike waved his NY Mets baseball hat in her direction.

"You need help with that?"

"No," Mike said. "I can do that myself," and he carefully slipped the hat over his little head.

"Perfect," Emma said. "You look like you're all ready to go to school now."

"Wait! I need to get my school bag," Jasmine shouted and disappeared back into the house.

"Did your Mommy pack your lunch bag?" Emma asked Mike.

"No, Daddy usually does that."

Meanwhile, Katie was rolling down Wilson Street in her brand new Alfa, carefully maneuvering over the speed bumps. Ray pulled his car back into the driveway and stepped out.

"Don't worry about that, Emma, I got it. You go get some rest. We've got a long day ahead of us."

Emma was unable to turn down an offer to lay down for a few hours. Her fatigue was too overwhelming.

"Okay. Thank you so much for everything, Ray. I'll be back in your office by one o'clock. Is that enough time?"

"That's perfect, Emma. See you later."

"Bye, kids. Have a good day at school."

"Bye, Emma," Mike gave her a big hug.

"See you soon," Emma heard Jasmine shout from her room.

She hopped down the stairs of the porch and walked past the Bentley to her little house in the back; her sacred haven, at least when the police were not around.

*What an absurd night this was*, Emma thought as she turned the key to the door of her own little Craftsman. A cozy beige carpet covering a small living room with a fireplace welcomed her back.

*I hope I can figure this out soon so Aunt Nettie can rest peacefully.* Emma walked past the living room and the open kitchen niche, then continued into the bedroom. She dropped her handbag on a wicker chair in the corner and collapsed into her white English country style bed. There was no time or energy left to take off her clothes. She crept under the blanket and closed her eyes. Sleep came over her as if someone had dropped a large piece of lead on her head.

***

*Tap, tap, tap.* Emma was typing Ray's work into the Lenovo desktop PC as fast as she could. It was definitely not the newest. As a matter of fact, something had gone wrong with the IP configuration on this specific machine after Ray had downloaded a file about the Syrian uprising—he'd caught a virus. The internet had stopped working in his office altogether. When Ray finally changed the telephone company, the IP address stored in the old computer could not be removed. His computer was stuck on the address, and could no longer be logged on to any other internet connection. What a paradox! So while Ray was playing around on his MAC using high-end technology (provided he wasn't speaking rivers into his voice recorder), Emma was typing her fingers "to the bone," until they were sore and achy for hours after work, on a computer which could not be considered much more than a typewriter.

Frankly, she didn't care. She was happy she didn't have to decipher Ray's hand-typed notes. When the spool on his Underwood had run out of ink, he had temporarily switched to a more modern technology: dictation. *He should always do that!* Emma thought as she typed away. *Tap, tap, tap.* At the time, she hoped he would never find a store where they repair typewriters. Unfortunately, Ray knew of one. He just couldn't remember the exact address.

*Tap, tap, tap.* "I have to take a short break," Emma announced, safely surrounded by the huge brown office chair in which Ray had placed her.

"No problem, dear. Go right ahead." Emma took her earphones off and got up, leaving the chair swinging around its own axis as she took her leave for the restrooms.

When she came back, she heard voices. Someone must have entered the office very quietly. She was usually able to hear what was going on around the office from the bathroom. That's how she knew the property manager was Ray's son; he had entered while she was on break, and she heard them talking tensely.

It was not like the Craftsman houses had a tremendous amount of insulation incorporated in their walls.

The door to the office was half-open, and she could hear voices whispering low. She didn't want to interrupt, so she stayed in front of the door, motionless. Strangely, the office chair that she had left several minutes ago was still spinning.

Emma took a closer look. Somebody was sitting in the chair. The same person who was talking to Ray. The chair swung around faster and faster and then suddenly, it came to a violent stop.

Emma was staring into the stone-cold face of Natalie Woodbridge. Blood was streaming down her face. "Emma, help me!" she whispered. She was as dead as a tree log.

Emma shivered. Instinctively, she screamed, "Aunt Nettie!" She woke up with a start. Where was she?

***

*TAP, TAP, TAP*! Again? What was *that*, now? Somebody was at the door!

Emma was fully awake now. She crawled out from under the blanket, tearing herself away from her horrific nightmare. She noticed that she was still dressed, and she was shivering from what she had seen in her dream. Only half-conscious, she tucked her feet into a pair of slippers and walked to the door.

"Good afternoon, Miss Robinson! Is everything okay? I heard you screaming."

Lieutenant Savalas was standing in front of the door with a bouquet of mixed flowers in his hands. He was wearing his uniform, as usual. *A truly stunning man*, Emma thought as she looked into the handsome man's hazel eyes. Those were honest eyes, she knew. His brows were masculine and full, exactly the way she liked it. *He's got that look. He has the Sean Connery look.* Then she realized where her mind was taking her again, and refused the entire idea.

"Oh, it was nothing," Emma denied having any problem. "Just a nightmare. How...c-can I help you, Lieutenant?" she stuttered.

"I was wondering if you would like to go for lunch tomorrow. I would like to make up for the terrible night you must have had," Savalas improvised. He was astonished how the words just seemed to flow, without him thinking about any of this. Quickly, he pushed the flowers into Emma's hands as if to say: "I am done with them, now you deal with this!"

"Here!"

The truth was, he was beaming to see Emma.

Now that was weird. Emma protested. "But, isn't that...illegal? I mean, taking out a suspect in the middle of a criminal investigation?"

She looked at the flowers; they were just a mix of standard garden flowers, but she loved them. *He must not know how much I am into flowers*, she thought, and bent to inhale their scent. The smell was wonderful. "Oh, thanks, by the way!"

Savalas smiled from ear to ear. She hadn't turned him down. "No, it's okay," he fibbed. No way was he going to let her know that this was official.

"Besides, you're no longer a suspect, remember? Meet you at noon tomorrow?"

Emma was surprised. She was not the type who had fast answers for unexpected situations. They usually came the next day, when it was all too late.

"I'll have to ask Ray for a longer lunch break, but... Well, yes, I guess so!"

Savalas was very happy. He had forgotten all about the initial reason for showing up at her doorstep, and actually looked forward to going out with her.

Emma had almost closed the door when her slowly awakening brain made the connection. "Oh, if this is about the case..."

Savalas was already walking back to his car. Emma closed the door.

*Stupid policemen. They're all the same, corrupt and immoral. Your looks won't get you anywhere, Savalas*, Emma swore, rushing to the bathroom to finally take a shower.

# Interrogating Ray West

McGinnis was in a bad mood. In a little while, he was going to interview the Iranian guy.

Spending more time than necessary with people whose egos where taller than the Mount Everest and their benefit to society questionable was not really his concept of having a good day. He made sure he had all the facts together before he turned off his PC and left the old cubicle of an office to confront the lion.

***

Ray had just returned from his daily routine of delivering his kids to school, and was somewhat distracted.

"Good afternoon, Mr. Ginnis," Ray said as he opened the door of 987 Wilson Street. He attempted smiling, but didn't really succeed in bringing up the brightness that usually shone from his face. The events of the previous day had weighed on him heavily, and he did not look forward to this conversation. He knew that some of the events of his past were going to be uncovered, events that he had made peace with years ago. Ray didn't like to share his tragic family history with strangers.

"McGinnis, please," said the detective, annoyed. The mistake was happening way too often again, McGinnis noticed. Time to make progress in this case. It bothered him when intelligent people couldn't remember his name. They obviously didn't think it mattered.

"Oh, I'm sorry Mr. McGinnis, I wasn't paying attention. Please come in."

Ray let the tiger into the wooden wrath of the lion's cave. The light in the entrance hall was dimmed by the handcrafted stained-glass windows that enlightened the square room. The ceiling was low. A photograph of Ray and Katie's wedding, in sepia brown, decorated the hall. McGinnis knew that it was all brand new stuff made to look old. The house was over a hundred years old. It was just another piece of a vast cultural heritage, and a part of this town he was born into. McGinnis was proud to be a Pasadenan.

Ray West lived smack in the middle of it. It was the Bungalow Heaven Historic district. This area of Pasadena was not only renowned for its remarkable examples of historic Craftsman cottages, it was supposedly still a safe neighborhood. Although strongly denied by its inhabitants, crimes did happen here. This was probably good for only one person: Detective McGinnis. It kept him busy, and didn't allow him to spend any time thinking about his own family history.

***

The detective started to feel at home as soon as he walked through the door of the old Craftsman. He hated it when he felt that way; it disturbed the clarity of his view as an investigator.

"Follow me," Ray said and guided him into the living room.

The two men entered a room with a slightly higher ceiling. Unlike the hallway, the antique wood beams were visible in this room. Family photographs decorated the walls around a brick fireplace that obviously didn't get used too often. *Why waste money on an amenity you never use?* McGinnis secretly justified his decision to live in a cheap one-bedroom apartment, with no amenities except an air conditioner for the summer, a stove, an old ironing board, and a refrigerator.

"Those are the original wood beams from nineteen fourteen, when this house was built. The contractors sanded them down for three months, until they were restored to their original state. When I bought this house, there was white paint all over them," Ray explained proudly.

"I know, Mr. West. I grew up in this town. The houses here are all old. As a matter of fact, I grew up in an old Spanish house in Altadena. It's all nice and wonderful to live in an old house like that as long as they're well maintained.

In my case, we had some heavy rainfall one day, and the roof got a leak. My mother, who was a widow, could not afford to pay for the repairs. We soon had to evacuate, and almost give the house away—for a price that wasn't much more than a smack in the face."

"I understand, Mr. Ginnis." McGinnis gave Ray a look that spoke more than words.

"Sorry. McGinnis, of course. Water?"

"Yes, please," McGinnis said, unable to conceal the insulted tone in his voice.

The truth was that these old houses reminded him of his bad fate with his ex-wife. He was ready to overcome his harsh childhood experiences of poverty, and planned to purchase a house for his wife. He came home one day with a purchase contract in his hands, and entered their modern two-bedroom apartment to find a bundle of divorce papers laying on his desk. Lauren had been cheating on him with Alfio, a fashion model ten years younger, while McGinnis had been putting in overtime to make his wife happy with a Craftsman home. What a blow! And then the accident... No, no, McGinnis was done with the idea of ever moving back into a house. All done.

He moved on to study the family photos while Ray was in the kitchen getting water. It helped him take his mind away from his own horrific family history.

A photo of Ray and Katie in a silver frame hung above the fireplace. In it, Katie wears an airy dress, Mike is sitting cross-legged in front of his father, and Jasmine is hugging her mother. There's an older man in shorts smiling to Ray's left, and two women, apparently Katie's sister and her mom, on her right. A *fairly recent photo*, McGinnis concluded from the boy's age. Maybe taken a year or two ago, on a family visit to his wife's hometown.

Right below this one, another photo in a gold frame was of the same people, and a few years earlier. No kids, and Ray and Kate in wedding attire. Kate—considerably thinner at this point—was surrounded by her family; Ray was alone with his new trophy wife and his success.

On the brick mantel of the fireplace stood a black and white photograph of the much younger Katie, her hair set in a high wave, sixties style. The photo must have been taken around her graduation from high school. The soft skin of her teenage face was almost tangible through the glass. Next to Katie's senior picture were a portrait of Jasmine in a white dress and a baby picture of Mike, all framed in alternating gold or silver—to create a color theme, assumed McGinnis. He hated domestic perfectionism; it just proved that people with too much money did not have enough important things to do.

He moved on to the pictures on the wall: In a wooden frame marked with a black bow in the left-hand corner was the photo of a young Persian woman, leaning against an ancient pillar somewhere near a big mountain. The woman was pregnant. McGinnis wondered where it had been taken.

At this moment, Ray walked in. "Your water, McGinnis." *He can say it, after all*, the detective thought. He was almost thrilled. McGinnis took the glass and emptied it in one take. He didn't like to mess around. He dumped his empty glass on the heavy wooden antique salon table standing next to him.

"Your first wife?" McGinnis asked in a low voice, attempting to show some compassion.

Ray picked up the glass and slid a paper coaster under it, in order to avoid staining the valuable antique. McGinnis watched Ray take care of the antique with a painful feeling of disdain in his heart. He was grateful that he didn't have to worry about any valuables in his own apartment. On the worn out couch in his own place, he could just slump down and rest. That's all he needed. Here, he was afraid to touch anything at all. *What a hassle!* They were both standing.

"Yes, Mr. Ginnis. That is Hafa. Was," Ray said sadly.

"I'm sorry, Mr. West. That must have been a tough loss. Where was the photo taken, if I may ask?"

"In Persepolis. Hafa was six months pregnant at the time, and it was right before we moved to Beirut. I had been offered a job at the university there, as a lecturer on Persian culture and literature. We were very relieved when I was finally accepted at the university, because by changing jobs, I was able to evade the Iranian massacre. This was right around 1988, and we had decided to visit the historic city of Persepolis before we'd be gone for good. Living in Iran was not safe at the time, not for open minded people like me, Mr. McGinnis."

"So I've heard," replied McGinnis bluntly. He continued to study the vast collection of family photos and quietly made a note in the back of his mind to visit the cultural sight of Persepolis sometime when work was slow, and Bartholdo would send him on vacation. McGinnis never took any time off on his own. However, because he worked for the state, eventually they forced him. Also, he hoped that the political situation in the Middle East would be in a reasonable state by then, because he did not feel like getting himself kidnapped by some crazy fundamentalists during his vacation leave.

"And who is this?" McGinnis pointed to the picture of an adolescent boy. He was dressed all in black and would not have caught McGinnis' attention if it hadn't been for the boy's captivating looks.

"That's my son Assim, born from my first wife."

"How old is he now, if I may ask?" McGinnis had all the answers printed out on his desk table, but it was interesting to hear them spoken aloud.

"Assim is twenty-seven years old now, and he works as a realtor in Los Angeles. He moved here from New York where he was studying for his real estate license, only recently. When I told him that I had inherited another property, he moved out here to help me."

"How is your relationship with your firstborn son? I don't hear you talk about him all that often."

"We had...a lot of differences when he was an adolescent."

"That happens..."

"Yes, Mr. Ginnis." In the turmoil of the questions, Ray had unconsciously given up on the use of the suffix, much to the detective's chagrin. He was tired of correcting him.

"But in our situation, things became *very* difficult after my wife passed away. As you might know, Hafa was one of the victims who got killed by the Israeli "Operation Grapes of Wrath" on April 18th, 1996. She was helping out on the UN compound. What happened there was very, very unfair. And Assim, my son, who was only eight at the time and just starting to think, had a very hard time forgiving the Israelis for this assault on a camp of innocent refugees. The predominantly Muslim friends that Assim had at the time did not necessarily help the situation. They were anti-Semitic, if you know what I mean. God bless Yitzhak Rabin. He was a true peacemaker. The fundamentalists who were responsible for his assassination in November 1995 caused the peace movement between Israel and Palestine such a setback; the world has not recovered from it until this day. May his soul rest in peace."

"Aha, interesting. So you resent the assassination of Yitzhak Rabin?"

"I pity it, very much so. The man was a peacemaker, a great politician. The signing of the Oslo Accords was a revolutionary step forward in the peace movement, at the time."

"Please correct me, if I'm wrong: Yitzhak Rabin was killed by his own people, a group of Jewish fundamentalists. Is that correct, Mr. West?"

"You did your homework, Mr. Ginnis. That's correct." McGinnis gave himself a high-five.

"Actually, I remember this event like it was yesterday. I was driving back from a dinner date with my deceased ex-wife when the radio announcer suddenly went silent, then reported Mr. Rabin's assassination. This was one of few good moments between my ex and me—our relationship had started to fall apart long before—but when the announcer spoke about Yitzhak Rabin's death, a long silence fell between us. It was the beginning of the failure of the Oslo Accords. Just like our relationship failed shortly after. But I will never forget that moment," the detective shared humbly.

"You are also a widower, Mr. Ginnis?" Ray inquired carefully.

"Yes, Mr. West. That's a story you don't want to hear. But I'm very easily able to relate to losing a loved one. So that brings me to my next question: how did you feel about the loss of your wife?"

Ray took a deep breath. The detective was doing his job well. He was using the emotional approach. This was exactly what Ray had been afraid of. He had not spoken about Hafa in a long, long time, and he did not wish to be reminded of the tragedy.

"As you can imagine, it was not easy. As a single father in a predominantly Islamic culture, it was difficult for me to show Assim my values. Assim was a teenager and at that time, our children begin seeking their independence by having friends—a very important stage in anyone's development toward maturity. Unfortunately, as I said, many of Assim's friends were angry with Israel, and conservative in their views. No matter how often I told him that governments do not make the people, and that his mother would not have liked the type of friends that he was seeing, Assim continued to withdraw from me. When I got the job at Caltech in the U.S. and started dating Karen, he refused to come to the States with me because of our conflicting worldviews."

"Interesting," stated McGinnis. "And what made him change his mind, after such extreme measures? Judging from the family photos, he didn't attend your second wedding."

Ray reflected. "Money? The prospect of obtaining a real estate license and wanting to make a quality living, I assume," said Ray sadly.

"Well, that plan worked out. Where is Assim right now, if I may ask? I might have some additional questions to ask him about your family history and the events that happened yesterday. As your property manager, I assume that he has free access to all of the houses—which, unfortunately, makes him a prime suspect."

"Yes, he does," Ray confirmed. "But I don't have his personal address."

"Really?"

"No, I don't. As I told you, we are not close that way. But I have his office address. Wait a minute; he gave me his card."

Ray walked through the room and then opened what must have been his personal office. He came back with Assim's card.

"This is his office address and phone number. You can call him here."

McGinnis studied the card: Corson Street. Fancy. That was smack in the business center of the old part of town, where all the law offices were located. *The guy must be good at whatever he's doing*, figured the detective.

"And regarding yourself, Mr. West, it sounds like your own alibi is bulletproof. Either you have a lot of very good friends who would risk their integrity for you, or you are telling the truth. So far no one at the theater has confirmed anything else but your presence there."

That forced a chuckle out of Ray's otherwise serious composure. "Both things are true, Mr. Ginnis. I do have very good friends, but I am also definitely *not* a murderer. I think deep inside, you know that."

McGinnis shrugged. "As a crime investigator, I have been trained not to trust anybody until the guilty party is found."

"I see." Ray was getting tired of dealing with this old rhinoceros of a person.

"Thank you, Mr. West. That would be it for the moment. I appreciate your taking the time to talk about all this. I know this must not have been easy for you."

"No problem. Come again if you need anything. All you have to do is knock on the door."

"Thank you. I'll keep that in mind." McGinnis lifted his newsboy hat and went looking for the door. He'd had enough. The Craftsman and the writer were making him nauseous. He needed some fresh air.

"Let me walk you to the door, Mr. Ginnis."

"Don't bother; I'll find it."

Ray didn't let the rhinoceros go until he had properly walked him out. As someone who had also lost the love of his life, though in a different way, he felt some form of compassion for the detective. Ray opened the door for him.

"Goodbye, Detective."

"Good day!" McGinnis lifted his hat and was out. Wow, it had been getting sticky in there. An old loner, he couldn't handle too much family atmosphere.

No matter how much he disliked the writer, Ray West was probably not the murderer. He had a new lead, though; that brightened up his lousy mood to some extent.

McGinnis hated sitting on unsolved cases for too long.

# Friendly Conversation

Ray was tapping his fingers on the Mahogany desk, an expensive piece of luxury he had gifted to himself as a reward for the publication of his book. The office was a rather small room—an annex of the living room—that could be closed off with a specially installed pocket door. He rolled back and forth in his huge, brown office chair, feeling like a big shot.

It was one o'clock in the afternoon, and Emma was still not there. That was unusual. Emma was the living definition of the word reliable. Even if he had acquitted her of work for the morning, finding him at his office in the afternoon meant one o'clock post meridian in unspoken business terms. He wondered if he needed to be worried about her. Not that the events of the past day had left him cold, but there was just nothing he could do about them. He hoped that the night in jail had not caused the young woman any more trouble than necessary.

***

One brief look at her Tissot told her that she was definitely going to be late today. It was a quarter to one. Dressed in her undies, and a blouse covering her tired body—the remainders of the past days' wardrobe—she picked up the flowers from the kitchen table and dumped them into a vase.

Emma placed the flowers on a round wooden table in the living room. It was one of her trophies of what she called 'street shopping,' an item that some spoiled person had put out for pickup on one of the streets of Bungalow Heaven. She had been lucky that day; the owner was working in his yard. When she passed by, she asked him if she could have it, and he told her he would bring it to her house with his van. Now she had a dinner table, but no chairs to fit it. Still, she was happy she had it. Emma was a collector of valuable items. If she was ever able to get a better job, she might be able to purchase a home some day. Right now, that just wasn't possible. She would at least have to be able to cover the amount of the mortgage, if she didn't want to run out of money right away. But she could start out with collecting furniture.

Satisfied with the result on her table, she peeled off the rest of her clothes on her way to the bathroom and hopped in the shower. The cold water dripping on her bed-warmed skin woke her up. She washed her hair quickly and got out. A good scrub with a soft towel got rid of the last remainders of zombie world, and made her feel like a human being again. She rushed into the bedroom and picked out what work clothes she could find in this mess: a brown pair of business pants and another white blouse. While she pulled the clothes over her body, Emma was again surprised by how she always seemed to manage to have some sort of business wardrobe. It was not so with casual clothes. Countless were the days on which she wanted to spend a free weekend day, and she got stuck in her bedroom longer than she wanted because she couldn't find anything comfortable to wear. She usually wound up in the same old jeans and T-shirt look she had worn for decades. Something that flowed in the wind, like a blouse, a skirt, a scarf, or a dress, would be nice for a change.

But when Emma tried dresses on in the shops, there was usually something wrong with them. She just didn't feel like shopping for clothes, and it was pretty much the last point on her long to-do list. So right now, she felt lucky that she didn't have to dress for a day off. She could just postpone being herself for a couple of hours once more, by working for Ray.

Still, the stress of what she was going to wear when she was to go for lunch with Savalas was already haunting her. Luckily, it was probably also not much more than a business conversation. *So I might not bother thinking about it at all*, Emma decided as she slipped into her flats, grabbed her handbag and left. Knowing McGinnis, he had probably sent the good-looking lieutenant to find out some more about the case. Of course, she would never admit how indescribably disappointed she was about this, not even to herself.

She hadn't been asked on a date since she had left her boyfriend in New York. Of course, Savalas was with the police, so he was an off personality. She would have to put in some extra effort, and find out other ways of meeting someone. Then another wave of sadness bowled her over, because she remembered how Aunt Nettie had been her go-to person for all these topics. Now, Emma had to figure all these things out by herself. *What a horrible person they had to be, to have done this to her.*

The clothes from the previous day were scattered all over her living room floor. She quickly picked them up and threw them over a chair as she rushed across the room to the front door. *Lucky I'm not in a relationship*, she thought. *Who on earth would ever put up with this chaos?* she wondered, as she glanced at her Tissot. It was ten after one! Ray must be expecting her.

***

When she had a work assignment with Ray, Emma didn't have to ring the bell. Most people felt so safe in Bungalow Heaven they left their doors unlocked, and apparently so did Ray, even after the murder. Unfortunately, it looked like the lock on the door had not been an obstacle for the one who killed Aunt Nettie. It was either he had forced his way in after Emma had gone to Nettie's house, or the person had already been inside, waiting. Emma strongly favored the second hypothesis.

Ray was not one to intimidate easily. Even with his kids and family, what had happened to Aunt Nettie had not raised his personal concern. He had been in way more dangerous situations, at least from his perspective.

On Ray's porch, Emma tried the door. It was open, as usual. Respectful as she was, Emma had left her shoes on the porch for a while until the wood floors started ripping up her tights. Still hesitating, she decided to leave her shoes on today. Walking into a job with bare feet felt awkward. Emma wore no socks or tights on most days since she had come to California. It was just too hot.

"Welcome back!" Ray greeted her from his big-shot chair as Emma slid the office door open. "You feeling any better now?" he asked. His sweet Iranian accent forced a smile out of her exhausted figure. *Baby language*, she thought and immediately, she felt in the right place.

"A lot better," Emma said.

"That's good, because I have a lot of work for you. I have been speaking to the voice recorder all morning. You can type it up in Farsi, but once you're all done with it, I want you to translate the *Thoughts* into English. I haven't decided yet, but I might consider sending the script to the publisher in English directly.

If I do it in Farsi, I have to do the publication via my old Lebanese publishing house, and that feels very complicated. If the public likes *Thoughts*, I can still translate the English version back into Farsi, or use the notes that you've already typed up."

"Well, that makes a lot of sense to me. I have a question, though." "Go right ahead!" For some strange reason, Ray was in an awfully good mood. Emma couldn't understand that, after what had happened the previous day. Maybe he was just happy he hadn't been arrested.

"Do you have any idea who did it? You seem so joyful; I don't understand."

"Oh, my dear. I am not joyful over what has happened, not at all. I'm just focused on other things right now. In part, to get my mind off the horrible events, for I have seen enough bad things in my life. But to answer your question, no. Unfortunately, I have no idea who did it."

"Aren't you concerned about your children? You're not even locking the doors!"

Ray took a moment to think about this. "Not really, Emma. It doesn't seem to me that they are after my children, or me. If anyone wanted to get my family or to me, they would have done so long ago. As for the solving of the case, I'm letting the police handle it—and you should, too."

Ray gave Emma a warning glance from above his horn-rimmed eyeglasses. "I don't want anything to happen to you."

Emma considered his words. The first thing that jumped into her mind was Ray's son. What was his name again? He had the keys to all the houses and backhouses. She didn't understand why nobody even mentioned him. However, she also didn't think her security was at stake.

"What about the property manager, Ray? Aren't you concerned that he might have something to do with the case?"

"Assim?"

Emma nodded. Ray considered the question. "No."

"But why not?"

"Because Assim is my son. He had some trouble in his teenage years, I'll admit. But ever since he came to the United States and went into real estate, he cleaned up beautifully."

Smug as can be, Ray sank a little bit deeper into his office chair. "Why doesn't he ever show his face? It seems like he's playing a game of hide and seek with that rent check mailbox."

"He's probably just very busy, Emma. He has other properties to manage."

"I see."

Emma was perturbed. Ray noticed, but he did not understand why. As much as Ray understood about the problematics of women in a society still mainly governed by men, there were certain things about women that he would never understand—like Emma's reaction to Assim. And how could he? Assim was a male, strong and dangerously good-looking, and about her age. She was a woman; *of course* Assim's existence perturbed her.

"Can we get to work now?" Ray raised his eyebrows. She nodded.

# Assim Esfahani

The weather had changed. The sky was a menacing gray, and it was only a question of time until it would pour down in buckets. McGinnis kept staring at the property manager's business card that Ray West had handed him. He was back in his office and before he did anything, it was thought through. He made a brief mental summary of the case so far.

The list of possible suspects was complete. McGinnis knew if the assassination of Miss Woodbridge had been a common armed burglary, her house would have been looted by the time the police arrived; so he concentrated his case on finding suspects among her nearer acquaintances. Miss Woodbridge had no relatives, so her surroundings had to be defined by the people she had been dealing with on a daily basis: Emma Robinson, Ray West, his family, the property manager, and the couple from the backhouse.

Now that Lieutenant Savalas would be making an in-depth assessment of Emma's knowledge on the following day, the two things remaining to do were to get in touch with Alan Foster and Maureen Dorsay (who should be back from their trip to Arkansas by now) and set up a meeting with the property manager. McGinnis had a funny feeling about both parties, and his feelings usually turned out to be true.

So all in all, the rhinoceros was semi-content, which meant he was in a fairly good mood compared to most other days. Barthold Meane walked past his office cubicle, which was closed off by a glass wall, the window blinds closed as usual. *Knock knock.* Meane did not bother to await the answer, which he knew would never come.

"Got anything new on the case, McGinnis?" He stepped in uninvited.

"Nothing new, Chief, but the suspects have been rounded up. I'm sure by the end of the week, the case will be resolved–if nobody interferes." By nobody, he meant Bartholdo. If anyone was going to disturb the natural resolution of the case, McGinnis was sure it would be Barthold Meane. If not for him, solving this case was going to be a picnic.

"Excellent job, McGinnis. Give me a list of the suspects."

"Of course," McGinnis almost snarled. Meane turned on his heel to leave McGinnis' cubicle as quickly as he had arrived. A copy of *Flames* was dangling from his left hand.

"How's the book?" McGinnis, at least, wanted to know.

"Best thing I've read in years," Bartholdo said. "You should read it, McGinnis! It will get your mind off all the crime and make you think of better things."

"Forget it, Bartholdo." McGinnis replied. "Never."

"Bring me that list. I want to see if there's anything I can do to help accelerate the resolution of the case. We got the *L.A. Times*, the *Pasadena Star News*, the *New York Times*, and all those guys waiting for an answer. I have a press conference scheduled for Friday. It would be good if the case could be resolved by then."

"Of course, Bartholodo. I'll will see what I can do."

McGinnis made a quarter turn to the left in his medium sized office chair and activated the computer screen with a gentle stroke over the keyboard. Yes, McGinnis was capable of gentleness. That's why he was working for the good guys, he assumed.

With a crooked smile on his face, he typed a few words into the empty Word document, starting with an order:

```
Do not contact. Main suspect.
McGinnis's dirty work will do.
Signed: PMcG
```

*Control P.* McGinnis grabbed the freshly printed paper and brought it to Bartholdo's office. Of course, Bartholdo was not there. McGinnis did not even need to glance over to the kitchenette where Bartholdo was sitting, legs up, a cup of coffee at his side, poring over the highly acclaimed piece of literature.

*Goddamn fool*, McGinnis cursed silently. He dropped the paper on Bartholdo's desk before walking back into his own office.

***

McGinnis hung up the phone. An almost goofy-sounding friendly male voice spoke on the other line. If that other person handled customers in real estate, they couldn't afford not to be friendly.

After half a day wasted at the office, McGinnis finally arose from his desk. Too many hours spent in that windowless cubicle with lousy air had not only ruined his marriage, but his waistline as well. McGinnis was lucky he had Nell. She didn't care about superficial things like that.

Well aware of the recent lucky strike he had made in his love life, McGinnis preferred to have lunch at Souplantation, where he could load up on some vitamins and save some calories.

He needed to get some food into his empty system before he approached his next suspect. He didn't want to give anything away unintentionally just because he was suffering from an acute case of hypoglycemia, so he piled on the dressing.

***

Back in his car, McGinnis made a right turn onto Corson Street at St. Andrew's church, a stylistic homage to the Giotto tower on St. Marc place in Venice, Italy. St. Andrew's was one of Pasadena's main historical landmarks.

A brick office building with black tinted windows welcomed him coldly.

Even though this building had certainly been executed with perfection on an architectural level, McGinnis loathed its concept: in his opionion its tinted windows were a reflection of the shady businesses that were being conducted on the inside, eternally protected from legal pursuit by an army of Ivy League lawyers, but unaffordable to the majority of an uneducated, and clueless public. Plus, the lean choice of bricks in this modern building ruined the whole magic of the traditional baked stone for him, which gave the old town its special flair. But like it has been mentioned before, the detective had his very own set of world views.

A huge sign was posted in front of the entrance court, a landscaped garden designed to provide pleasure outside to an absent office community. With golden letters the sign announced the main occupant of this gloomy building: "Luminus–International Trust". But that's not where McGinnis was headed. He entered the ground floor through glass double doors, walking into an ornate lobby with polished marble floors and golden elevator buttons.

*Ding*; the elevator arrived. Nobody inside. *Of course not. They're all sitting in front of their laptops, Macs, and PCs typing up new legal concepts for the world that better never be.* McGinnis pressed three. *Ding.* He exited into a hallway facing the entry of a large legal corporation.

Adon & Co. was the name above the doorway. A secretary with straight, perfectly shiny brown hair, perfect makeup, and fake nails welcomed him.

"Good afternoon, Adon and Company, how can I help you?" The secretary was on the phone.

"Yes, please," she pushed the transfer button and hung up.

He already knew that there was no way that the perfect secretary would ever acknowledge McGinnis' presence, so, he cleared his throat and interrupted her very important workflow. "I'm looking for Assim Esfahani from Esfahani Properties, please," McGinnis said with the calmest voice ever, trying to conceal the hatred he felt for these pseudo-environments.

"You're looking for Assim?" she quickly said. The secretary's expressionless face brightened up for the fracture of a second. While she was convinced that nobody noticed her smirking expression, McGinnis most certainly did. "Yes, please," he said. He chose not to show his license because he did not want to interrupt the natural flow of actions, which would have been different if he had been wearing his uniform.

"Have a seat," the secretary advised him.

She picked up the intercom and dialed Assim's office. "There's someone here for you." She removed the phone from her face and covered the mouthpiece with her hand, addressing McGinnis. "Your name, please?"

"McGinnis. Detective McGinnis."

Unconcerned, she raised her eyebrows. "Police?"

McGinnis added, "Homicide." He watched her body shrink–the only moment when she lost the splendor of her perfect composure–with the hidden joy of a child eating forbidden candy. She quickly straightened herself out. McGinnis knew this body-shrinking behavior inside and out. He had seen it a thousand times, in every secretary he had ever dealt with. It was common body language, an expression of fear. It meant, *Can I get into trouble for being involved with a potential murderer, even if I didn't know he committed a crime?*

*And yes, you can,* McGinnis thought. *If you helped him concealhis actions, I could arrest you as an accomplice. But I probably won't, because no matter how pretty you are, you're not worth the trouble.*

"A Detective McGinnis is here for you. He says he's from homicide."

"He will be here for you in a moment," she said to McGinnis and hung up the phone, three degrees less confident than before he had introduced himself.

She nervously started clicking away with the mouse over a blank screen, pretending to be working. McGinnis knew she was not actually doing a thing.

***

A friendly-looking young man in casual clothes, wearing a gold necklace around his strong neck dashed around the corner. McGinnis envied the young man's swiftness, and the visual results of his obviously regular workouts.

The years of experience in the criminal investigation had not only physically put weight on him, but also spiritually: the amount of human knowledge and dark experiences weighed on his soul.

How much McGinnis would have given to be young and free of knowledge, like this clean-cut looking fellow!

"Mr. McGinnis?" McGinnis nodded. This was certainly not Assim. A man who thought himself as important as Assim would never get out of his office chair, McGinnis knew. The location of his office showed how much Assim must have thought of himself. Other agents rent booths out of real estate corporations. This guy needed a desk in a legal office, surrounding himself with more prestigious people, away from the pressure of the competitive real estate world. Pseudo-prestige.

"I'm Anselm, Assim's assistant. Come with me, Detective."

Just as swiftly as the young fellow had appeared, they rushed past a labyrinth of office cubicles and bookshelves filled with law books that no one would ever open up. It was all just for display, to make a good impression on the customer. The only difference between a corporate law office and a movie set was that criminals here actually landed in jail.

"Here we are." Anselm opened the door to a small corner office, overlooking the Old Town of Pasadena. Assim was on the phone.

"So the check bounced?"

McGinnis looked around. He spotted a poster-sized photograph of the Lakers versus the Portland Trailblazers. Basketball.

"It's a cashier's check for you, from now on."

Furious, Assim threw the phone on the hook. "Idiots!"

He looked at the phone rather than at McGinnis, who was curiously taking in the picturesque atmosphere of this very neat corner office.

"Detective Peter McGinnis," Anselm introduced him.

"Oh, I'm sorry. Good afternoon Mr. Ginnis. How can I help you?" Assim reached out his hand, decorated with golden rings on every other finger. *Pathetic.* From his corner position, he didn't even bother to get up. McGinnis ignored him and continued taking in the atmosphere. *All very neat*, he had to admit. Assim was a handsome fellow—well built, good features. McGinnis figured he must have women chasing him like wild prey, and unwillingly he was reminded of Alfio, his ex-wife's boyfriend, who was now out on parole.

Assim nonchalantly raised his plucked eyebrows, surprise on his pampered, pretty face, and pulled back his hand. He was wearing a white linen shirt and beige linen pants. *Big shot*, McGinnis couldn't help thinking.

"Have a seat."

McGinnis was looking askance at a small plastic chair, obviously a last-minute addition, between the two desks. McGinnis sighed and dropped his heavy body into the too small frame.

Squeezed in between the two desks, McGinnis continued to look around. Anselm meanwhile was sitting at his desk, near the south window, typing something up that looked like a rental lease. He pretended to ignore what was going on behind him, but McGinnis could feel him listening. McGinnis was very uncomfortable, but staying on his feet was just too much effort. He wasn't staying in here long, that was for sure.

"How can I help you?" The goofy voice from the corner position asked. Assim threw him an equally goofy smile that vanished as quickly as it had appeared.

"I am here with respect to one of your clients—her passing, specifically." The words hit home. Did he perceive a slight shiver passing through the assistant's body, or was McGinnis just imagining things? The typing from the south side of the room stopped for a moment.

"Mrs. Natalie Woodbridge, the tenant who lived on your father's property, was brutally slain Sunday. Somebody hit her over the head with a menorah. Death was instantaneous. We are still waiting for more details from the forensics department, but we have reason to believe that there might have been the anti-Semitic motive behind this case. Mrs. Woodbridge was a very peaceful and rather popular old lady."

Anselm continued typing, slowly. *Tap, tap, tap, tap...*

"And how does that lead you to me?" Assim maintained his nonchalant attitude, but some of the goofy had disappeared from his voice.

"As my research revealed, you are the property manager over there. You collect the rent each month, plus you have all the keys. This makes you a prime suspect."

Assim started to laugh. "Me? Murder an old lady?"

"Yes, Mr. Esfahani." McGinnis was not in the mood for fooling around. The space was too narrow, for one thing.

"Let's just get to the point: where were you Sunday night between 11 PM and 1 AM?"

"I was at the gym. Correct, Anselm?"

Without turning around, Anselm started to nod. "Yup!"

McGinnis shifted around in the too small chair. He was not only uncomfortable, he was starting to get annoyed as well.

"Isn't the gym closed at night?" McGinnis hadn't worked out in a while and was not quite up to date on the current practices of modern fitness clubs.

"Twenty-four-hour fitness. They're open twenty-four seven."

"Which location did you train at on that day? I assume that your club is a larger cooperation with several locations."

"I work out on Colorado Street."

"Do you have any kind of proof?"

Assim thought for a moment. "Anselm. He lives with his parents, so I let him stay at my place sometimes. He saw me leave and return."

Stunned, Anselm turned around in his chair and stared first at Assim, then at McGinnis. His innocent swiftness had been replaced with an expression of stress and fear. McGinnis knew the expression. He had seen it a thousand times.

"Correct."

"I see."

McGinnis couldn't sit there any longer. He needed to get up. His whole body was starting to ache. He was getting too old for this type of game. He got up.

"I'll have the department check your alibi. You got any travel plans?"

Assim shrugged. "Me? No. I'm not goin' anywhere. Why?"

"You are advised to stay in town until your alibi is cleared."

"Oh!" The goofy was back in his voice. Assim was feeling invincible again.

"Goodbye!"

McGinnis tipped his newsboy hat and walked to the door.

"Anselm!" Assim reminded his assistant to help him out the door. "No worries, Mr. Esfahani. I'm a grown man. I can find my way out here on my own."

Relieved, Anselm stayed in his chair. He didn't want to confront the detective any more than necessary.

McGinnis was almost out the door when he turned around one more time. "You a Laker's fan, Mr. Esfahani?"

"Portland Trail Blazers. Why?"

"Interesting. I'd have thought you were for the Laker's." McGinnis tipped his hat again and left.

If McGinnis had left his ears in the office, a huge sigh of relief would have been heard upon his exit, he knew. An even larger question mark would have been written across the troubled young assistant's face.

# Lunch with a Cop

It was Wednesday morning, and Emma didn't know whether she was getting ready for work or for a date. Lieutenant Savalas was supposed to pick her up at noon. What a cheap trick that old detective had played on her, sending a sexy cop to get some information out of her. *No way! I'm not dressing up for anything,* she decided. Emma slipped on her usual blue business slacks and a white blouse. She checked her outfit in front of the bedroom mirror. *This works!*

A pair of black ballerina flats and gold hoops completed her outfit. Her hair was in a low ponytail, and she wore barely a trace of makeup on her face—just some mascara that she'd lightly and carefully brushed on her lashes. Natural was Emma's best look.

***

Emma's day at the office was rather tedious. Ray had done a lot of preparation work overnight, and Emma could barely keep up with the typing. He was planning to finish the first series of his *Thoughts* by the end of the week. For Emma, that meant a lot of brainwork; half of it was in Farsi, and Emma had to translate on the go. *Tap, tap, tap.* While Emma was typing, Ray paced up and down the extended office area and the living room, sheltered by hundred-year-old wood-beams.

Ray stopped mid-stride. *Tap, tap, tap. Tappity-tap.* Ray turned around abruptly. A touch on her right shoulder tore Emma out of her typing meditation. She couldn't hear him through the big headphones that she had plugged into the audio device. Emma pressed stop on the audio. She did not bother to look up, leaving her hands on the keyboard, ready to tap on as soon as Ray was done with what he had to say.

"Whatever happened to that typewriter ribbon I sent you out for, Emma? Do you still have it or did it get lost in the procedure?"

Emma dropped the audio, and her headphones fell on the floor. "Of course: the ribbon!"

She picked up her Native American-style handbag and placed it on Ray's table. She looked at him; he looked back.

"Do you mind?" Emma asked.

Ray made a move forward with his chin as if to say, "Go on, girl!"

Emma picked up her handbag and dumped the entire contents onto Ray's desk.

A huge pile of random objects dropped onto his workspace. A tampon rolled off his desk. Embarrassed, Emma made a dive to pick it up. Ray didn't flinch. He was married for the second time, things like that didn't put him in any distress.

"Oops!" She got it and stuffed it back into the zipper compartment of her huge bag. He grinned for a fraction of a second. Then his face went serious again, just in time for Emma not to notice how amused he was.

Having regained her composure, Emma looked at the pile.

"Let's see." A green leather wallet, a key chain with a teddy bear on it, a packet of tissues, at least five pens, scrap paper...

From the somewhat logical chaos emerged a small plastic bag that contained the desired object. It had been covered up by the tissues.

"Here it is!" Emma grabbed it and handed it to Ray.

Ray was impressed; this little bag of nothing had survived the night of prison and all the turmoil.

"You know how to install it?" Emma asked.

"I've done it a thousand times. A lifetime of experience, so no worries." Ray grabbed the ink spool and went to the typewriter, on a separate table in the office off to one side. He started to threadit in. Seconds later, Emma heard one snap, two snaps, and he was done.

"I'm going to type some more *Thoughts* down while you work with the audio. Save time."

"Sure thing," Emma said. She had just finished packing all the contents back into her handbag, and was about to put the headphones back on when the doorbell rang.

"Who's that?" Ray asked, clueless.

*I think I know who that is*, Emma thought, somewhat embarrassed. Before she could do anything to save herself, Ray had already walked up the door.

***

Lieutenant Savalas was standing there in full police gear. He was holding a bouquet of flowers in his hands.

"Lieutenant?" Ray was utterly confused. He was rather familiar with the procedures of the police, but this was strange. Was the Pasadena Police Department better than he thought? A glimpse of hope arose in the skeptic author.

Savalas was also slightly caught off guard. The words he had intended to say couldn't make it past his throat. Ray had to help him out.

"Are those for me?" He teased him.

That was enough to break the ice. Savalas chuckled.

Wow! Ray was impressed. *Human after all.* There was a glimpse of hope for the city of Pasadena.

Meanwhile, Savalas got his voice back. "For Miss Robinson." That's as much conversation as Savalas was capable of at this moment. It seemed he was more nervous than he had expected.

"Oh!" Ray shook his head. How did he not think of that?

Apparently, he was getting old.

Emma was already standing behind him with her handbag, hoping to spare everyone from any further embarrassment—and before Ray could make any further sarcastic comments.

"I'm taking my lunch break, Ray. I'll try to be back by one." Quickly, Emma walked onto the porch, closely followed by Savalas.

Ray just stood there, stunned, and watched them walk away. He closed the door.

"Lovebirds. Really?"

He shook his head and walked back to his typewriter.

***

"More flowers?"

Confused, Emma smelled the lovely bouquet. Savalas nodded as he handed them to her.

"I just didn't want to make you uncomfortable with my appearance at your boss's door," Savalas fibbed again.

"They're beautiful!"

Savalas extended his elbow. "Arm?"

Emma hooked hers into his, and together they marched off the famous writer's porch.

"Wait a minute," Emma said, as they headed for the police car.

"Don't worry, Emma, I'm not going to arrest you. We're only driving to a restaurant."

Emma giggled. "No, it's not that. Let me quickly put these flowers into a vase. They're too beautiful to let them go bad."

"Oh." Savalas snickered. "Sure. While Savalas waited in front of his car, Emma rushed into her little haven, hidden behind Ray's house.

Inside, she went to the kitchen and looked through all her cabinets for another vase. She found one and took it out to see if the flowers fit. The bouquet fit perfectly. Powder, water, flowers, doily—place it on the living room table, and done. She would cut the stems later. Emma took a step back and looked at her colorful table. That's what had been missing in here. Flowers!

She took another quick sniff of the lovely scent, threw one last glance into a small wall mirror, and sighed as usual. She was not perfect at all, but she looked okay. It was astonishing that a guy like Savalas would want to go out with her. *Besides, this 'date' was set up by McGinnis, anyway, to get more information out of me,* Emma reminded herself as she locked the door.

When she came back to the car, Savalas was still standing there, holding the door open. He was a gentleman, Emma could tell.

"All done?" he smiled.

"All done!" Emma said and hopped into the car. Savalas got in from the other side. He calmly strapped himself in, then sighed. He turned his head to Emma. She looked back. Their eyes met for a fraction of a second. It was a brief moment in time that lasted just a tiny bit longer than it should have.

Savalas turned his head away. He finally spoke. "Off to Gustavo's?"

"Sounds good to me," Emma said.

Savalas started the car and made a U-turn before driving up the street.

Emma complained. "Hey, that's illegal!"

Savalas sighed again. "Not all the state's laws are practical, or doable. A standard police officer probably breaks the law between one to three times per day. The trick is to pick the ones that are insignificant."

"Insignificant? When I make a move like this, I have to pay several hundred bucks for breaking the law!" Emma protested.

"Making a U-turn on a residential street where there is no traffic or car in sight is insignificant. Shooting a man just because he has a different skin color or religion is *very* significant, and not at all recommended."

"Oh." Emma sighed.

"That's where I'm coming from," Savalas justified his illegal move.

"I see," Emma remembered who had gotten her into the police car in the first place. Even if officially it was just for a date, her mood dropped considerably when she remembered her situation.

***

They drove quietly for a while. They were climbing the hill on Lake Street, then they crossed Washington Boulevard, still with no more words spoken. Savalas pulled onto a side street and parked. He cut the motor and hurried to Emma's side.

She gracefully stepped out. "Thank you!"

She was heading to the restaurant directly, but Savalas stopped her.

She was confused. "What's the matter?"

Savalas reached deep into his soul. "I am so sorry for your loss," he said. He opened his arms and wrapped them around Emma's soft body for a big, long hug.

This cop was surely walking around with a good bag of tricks! Before she knew it, she was sobbing uncontrollably in his strong arms.

"I am sorry our system made you go through all this. Like losing a loved one isn't hard enough, on an honest person like you."

Emma pulled herself together. "Did you find any more evidence?"

"We're working on it. They're checking out the family in the other back-house now, and McGinnis had a conversation with the property manager, whom

Ray West seems to be strangely protective of, for some reason. I don't know yet what came out of that."

Meanwhile, the two lovebirds had walked into the restaurant. A waitress seated them in an enormous, deep-cushioned booth. Emma tried to get comfortable, but she couldn't stop wondering about the progress of the case.

"The property manager?" Emma asked full of concern.

Savalas studied the menu. The waitress stood there waiting for their order.

"I'll have the seafood pasta and a dinner salad," Savalas ordered.

"A Caesar salad for me, please."

"Any drinks?"

Emma shook her head. "Just water, then," Savalas confirmed.

"All right then." The waitress walked away. Savalas was studying Emma's expression.

She didn't know whether to keep looking at the menu, or at the TV. Savalas was making her nervous.

"So what's up with the property manager?" Savalas insisted. "He good-looking or something?"

A cheeky smile rushed across Emma's face. "Why, is this an interrogation after all?"

Savalas chuckled. He knew that it was, sort of. Emma wasn't stupid. "I don't know!"

"What do you mean, you don't know? You've never seen him?"

The waitress brought their salads and waters.

"Just once, very briefly. It seemed that he was very well taken care of, but I couldn't say anything for sure. Aunt Nettie could have told you more about this."

"Oh yes? Natalie Woodbridge? Why?"

Savalas' pasta arrived, finally. He started to twirl the spaghetti around his fork. "She talked about him all the time!"

Emma was working on her salad between statements, eating heartily. "She wanted me to date him or something, but I never got to see him. He seemed to pick up the checks at random hours when nobody was around. Only Natalie seemed to catch him, mostly. Funny..."

"What's funny?" Savalas wanted to know.

"That last night, when I went to the movies with her, she was unusually quiet. I tried to cheer her up, and I mentioned the property manager, but nothing worked. She usually talked about him all the time, so I didn't understand what was going on. I thought she was getting ill, but she said she was okay. It was altogether a very strange night."

"You never mentioned that before," Savalas noticed as he was signing the check.

"I don't know, in all the turmoil, it must have escaped me. I haven't really thought about my last night out with her until just now."

"It's okay," Savalas calmed her. He got up, saying, "Arm?" Emma hooked in.

***

It was a quiet ride home, and Savalas had got just a little bit more information than he'd expected out of this fake date. McGinnis would be thrilled, and Savalas almost resented it.

He pulled up to the curb in front of Ray's house, and turned the motor off. "Hey, pretty lady. You ever want to do this again, maybe not during working hours?" Savalas held her arm tenderly.

Emma was unsure. This had all been too much again. "Can I think about it?"

Savalas let go of her arm. "Sure!" Emma smiled and got out.

"How about I give you a call at the end of this week, and see if I have anything positive to report on the case of Natalie Woodbridge?"

"Sounds good to me!" Emma said and walked away.

"Bye!" The Lieutenant waved and drove away.

Even though probably phony, it had not been such a bad date, Emma decided as she climbed the steps on Ray's porch. *A cop! I'm dating a cop! What a silly idea*, Emma thought.

# Catching a Blonde

Lieutenant Savalas was in his car, heading toward police headquarters on Garfield Street when his phone rang. He didn't need to check the display to figure out who it was.

"How did your interrogation go with the property manager, McGinnis? I heard some interesting information about him today."

"We need to check his alibi at the gym. Why, what did you hear?"

"Apparently the old lady had a crush on him or something. At least, she seemed to be talking about him a lot."

"I'm not surprised. He has the looks of an Adonis. What else should a bored old lady talk about?"

There he was again. Good old Detective McGinnis, nothing surprised him. Savalas thought that he'd found some seriouslyvaluable information. But no: he was only slightly frustrated.

"What about the flight arrangements? Any progress on that?" McGinnis wanted to know.

"I was just going to take care of that. But you have to understand, my appointment today had me stalled on that a bit."

"I do hope you had a good time," the detective snickered.

There was no comment.

"Let me know when you have anything."

"Consider it done." Savalas hung up and parked his car in his designated spot. He walked up the stairs to his windowless office, taking the stairs two at a time. Savalas wondered if McGinnis purposefully set up this lunch date thing just to get him together with Emma. McGinnis had some strange methods, and definitely couldn't be trusted.

*A date masked as an office inquiry?* He was going to have to confront McGinnis about that, Savalas mind-mapped, flinging open the door to the second-floor police offices. He didn't like to mix private affairs with work, and McGinnis was clearly doing that by planning for him to have lunch with Emma.

Settled in his small office, really a cubicle, he was not too excited about his current task. Savalas did not like office work. He was very glad his office work took up only a small percentage of his daily duties as a cop. Nevertheless, duty was duty; he picked up the phone and called the airline. He wanted to find out if Maureen Dorsay and Alan Foster had actually set foot on that plane.

Savalas was passed from customer service agent to customer service agent several times, then from manager to manager to manager. He faxed forms, authorizations, his police license, and other required paperwork to get an answer.

After being on the phone for over two hours, he finally got the information he was hoping to get out of this call. Alan Foster had boarded the flight to Arkansas, but his wife Maureen had not. The written confirmation of her absence on board pushed its way through the fax machine. They now had another murder suspect with blonde hair: Maureen Dorsay.

Trouble was up, Savalas knew that. He would now have to track down Maureen Dorsay. He still preferred getting out of the office and being in danger to sitting in an office doing paperwork.

Savalas was almost happy. He was going to get out today. He dialed McGinnis' number. *Where is he, anyway?* Savalas heard the phone ring from the cubicle next door. McGinnis was here in the office! Savalas threw the phone back on the receiver, and headed toward McGinnis' office. The detective was impatiently expecting him.

"So, was I right?" McGinnis asked, seated comfortably behind the cheap desk. He was chewing his upper lip, as he always did when he was thinking.

He tipped his hat, giving Savalas a friendly wave to step in.

Savalas nodded reluctantly as he walked into the equally windowless cubicle. *They could at least build a proper office for Pasadena's most important crime investigator,* Savalas thought. *Where do all those taxes that people pay every year go, anyway?*

"Dead right! Alan Foster took that plane to Arkansas, but Maureen Dorsay did not. How did you know that?"

McGinnis snickered, "Twenty years of experience in crime investigation helps you develop a certain instinct. It doesn't always reveal itself as truthful, but sometimes, as in this case, it does."

Savalas was impressed.

"Which leads you to your next job."

Savalas knew that he was going to have to find Maureen Dorsay. Because he did not know McGinnis that well, he was confused by the detective's strange attitude.

"Which is…?"

"Go find her and bring her here ASAP!"

"Of course. Consider it done." Savalas got up and went back to the quiet of his cubicle, with a big smile on his face.

McGinnis had given him a heads-up. He was sure that he had found the best lieutenant he was ever going to find. The only trick was to keep him here. Usually, the good ones eventually moved on to safer jobs, especially once they had a family. McGinnis had given him a big push in that direction today.

***

Back in his cubicle, Savalas wondered how he was going to find the suspect. He scrolled through her background file. He didn't recall seeing a car in the driveway when he picked up Emma.

*Bingo! Here it is. She works at Nestle, Glendale!* To be sure, he made a note of the woman's license plate and the make and model of the car. It was a burgundy Ford Escape. He decided to track her down at her job, and follow her from there.

Savalas grabbed his keys. Bounding downstairs at a pace of two steps at a time, he was back into the sunlight and fresh air in seconds. He got into his official police car and entered the 134, exited on Brand Avenue and headed north, then east, toward the Nestle Building. He parked in a regular space on the street to avoid attracting any attention. He walked into the fancy lobby with marble flooring and gold fittings. Savalas walked straight to the receptionist and presented his license.

"Does a Maureen Dorsay work here?" He asked. He wanted to have it confirmed that she was there before he caused a stir.

The receptionist, a heavyset, muscled Armenian guy, went through his online staff directory. He took his time. Savalas didn't care. He knew that the man would eventually provide him with the information.

"Marketing assistant in the advertisement department on the eighth floor, office number 808."

"Perfect! Thank you."

"Elevators are straight ahead to your left," the receptionist advised him.

Savalas turned and walked back outdoors. He glanced around to see if he could spot Maureen's SUV parked somewhere on the street. If not, he would have to patrol the parking garage. He decided that it was best to let her finish her daily routine and then catch her. It might bring in some additional information if he could catch her unawares.

One glance at the streets nearby revealed nothing. Savalas moved his police vehicle into the underground parking garage and parked near the exit. He got out of his car and informed the attending valet that he was patrolling for a person. The attendant cooperated quietly.

Savalas took a stroll through the parking garage in search of the burgundy SUV. With wise foresight, he'd brought a GPS device with him to attach to the SUV, so he could track the suspect even if she was not directly in sight. With the level of traffic at rush hour in Los Angeles, this tool was a must for any detective.

Savalas found her SUV in the middle of a full row on level P3. Savalas checked left and right. No one was in sight. He ducked down and attached the magnetic device onto the main beam of the SUV frame, under the driver's door. *No way will she ever figure out she's being followed!*

Relieved, Savalas walked back to his car and waited inside. He was prepared to leave as soon as the Ford Escape SUV showed up.

The day was almost over. The preparation of this catch had taken up his entire afternoon. It was now 4:30. Maureen should showup any minute.

***

Savalas waited and waited in the darkness of the parking garage. Finally, the first cars began to pull out of the dark cave of corporate America.

Savalas' day passed through his mind in retrospective. It began with some simple online paperwork in the morning. Paperwork seemed never to end, and there was never enough time for it. Then he'd made the stop at the flower shop for the bouquet, on his way to lunch with Emma. *Innocent and modest! She has no idea how beautiful she is.* Yes, he liked her—a *lot*. But there could be no dating until the case was over.

Meanwhile, a line had formed in front of the exit of the parking garage. *Sure enough! There it is!* The burgundy Ford Escape SUV came crawling up from the depths of the corporate cave.

Savalas remained quiet. The GPS was installed. He had time.

Slowly, the SUV approached the exit of the parking garage. Savalas saw a platinum blonde with dark sunglasses push a validation card into the parking machine. The SUV took off. Savalas started his motor. The GPS indicated that the SUV was heading toward the freeway.

Savalas drove slowly along, keeping an eye on the GPS. The SUV was going West on the 134, not to Pasadena. *Has Maureen been staying somewhere else while the investigation is taking place? That would explain why nobody has seen her until now.*

At the freeway intersection, the SUV changed lanes and headed north on Interstate 5, toward Sacramento. Maureen Dorsay was not going home.

Savalas' cell phone rang. He pressed the speaker button and checked the display. *Of course, it's McGinnis! Who else?*

"Has the suspect shown up yet, Savalas?"

"I'm right behind her on Five North. She's apparently not driving home."

"Excellent work, Savalas. Stay right behind her. Call me whenyou get close to the destination. I'll meet you there."

"But how...?"

McGinnis hung up. Once again, he was two steps ahead of Savalas. That was probably why he was the detective here.

Savalas kept following her. She went all the way past Burbank. Then her blinker went on, a half a mile before the Sheldon Street Exit. The SUV took that off ramp. Savalas dialed McGinnis' number.

"Suspect seems to be heading toward Sun Valley. I'm right behind her, McGinnis. What do you want me to do? Pull her over?"

"No. Maureen Dorsay is heading to Monica Brown's house, on Oneida Street in Sun Valley. Monica is her aunt. Apparently, she's been hiding out there for the past few days. I'm already parked at the house, just waiting for you and the suspect to arrive."

"Oh, I see. Well, I guess I'll see you in a minute."

There it was again! McGinnis was two steps ahead of him. Savalas just kept following the SUV.

When Maureen arrived at Monica's address, Savalas made sure he parked out of sight from the house, so she wouldn't realize she'd been followed. He could see McGinnis' Ford Futura in his rearview mirror. His car definitely wouldn't cause a stir in this neighborhood.

Savalas waited a bit to give the suspect time to enter the house. Then he got out and approached McGinnis' car. He gently knocked against the driver's window. McGinnis woke up, startled. He had put so much confidence in Savalas' timely arrival that he had fallen asleep.

"Ready, Detective?"

"Ready as spaghetti," McGinnis said and exited the car.

They approached the doorway of a simple green house probably built in the '60s. In front of the house, the grass was dried up and withered. Nobody was wasting any money on watering a garden here.

McGinnis rang the bell. Savalas shielded him.

A tired-looking middle-aged woman, with uncombed, gray hair, and a cigarette dangling from her mouth, opened the door.

"Whaddaya want?" she asked rudely.

McGinnis showed his badge. "We are from the Pasadena Police Department. We would like to speak to Maureen Dorsay, for routine questioning regarding the murder of one of her neighbors."

"Maureen's not here," Monica lied.

Savalas heard a loud noise coming from the back of the house.

Savalas and McGinnis exchanged a glance.

"Go!" McGinnis ordered, and Savalas ran back onto SheldonStreet, toward where the noise had come from.

"You know, I can arrest you for obstruction of justice, Miss Brown."

"I don't give a shit!" she said, and slammed the door shut, nearly scraping McGinnis' pretty nose. He snickered. What a character! But Monica Brown was not the person they were after.

A mere two seconds later, Savalas came back around the corner from Sheldon Street with Maureen in tow. She had tried to escape through the yard door. She was struggling to get away, but had no chance. Her hands were cuffed.

"Mrs. Dorsay, you are temporarily arrested for obstruction of justice. We have a few questions to ask you. You have the right to remain silent..."

Maureen looked McGinnis straight in the eye. "I want a lawyer!" Maureen protested.

"Everything in its time," he said calmly. He was nearly amused.

"Who's she riding with?" Savalas wanted to know.

"With you!" McGinnis advised and got back in his car. "See you at the station."

"Sure thing," Savalas confirmed. He was not looking forward to the drive back with this crazy woman.

"But what about my car? I need my car!" Maureen protested, as Savalas dragged her along the sidewalk to his police vehicle.

"Don't worry, lady! You'll get everything back in its own time. But right now, Detective McGinnis has a few questions for you," Savalas said. He shoved her into the back seat of his police car.

He was very happy that there was a barrier separating the back area from the front of the car. He didn't want to have too much to do with this dame.

Trapped in the police car, Maureen finally gave up her resistance and just stared out the window. Savalas got in the driver's seat and headed back to Pasadena. He turned the radio on loud to mask his discomfort with her sitting in the back seat.

# Interrogating Maureen Dorsay

Back at the police station, McGinnis was already sitting in the interrogation room with his newsboy hat placed on the table. He chewed on his upper lip as he waited impatiently.

McGinnis was astonished at how little native Angelinos knew about their own hometown. Lieutenant George Savalas was born and raised in Glendale and was intimately familiar with the local transit lines, but apparently he had no idea that it was faster to take the 210 Freeway during rush hour when coming from the valley. The young lieutenant still had a lot to learn.

McGinnis sat there for over twenty minutes before Savalas finally arrived with the suspect in tow. Savalas had been struggling to get her up the stairs. He was out of breath.

"Sit down, Mrs. Dorsay!"

Reluctantly, she dropped into the chair on the opposite side of the table, glaring at Detective McGinnis.

Nobody knew that Barthold Meane was watching them from behind the glass wall. Nobody cared that Meane never had anything to say during the official investigation process. He usually left the dirty work up to his lower officers, like McGinnis and Savalas. Since the interrogation with Ray West had not brought anything to light, Meane resolved to remain withdrawn in this case until some light was cast on the potential murderer. Of course, he would pressure them to bring the facts out faster, so he could hold a press conference at the end of the week. Until then, he remained silent behind the glass wall.

Savalas got quite a start when he walked into the observation room and saw Barthold Meane sitting at the desk, with his legs propped up on it as usual.

"Good evening, Mr. Savalas. I see you made some progress on the case," Bartholdo welcomed him from inside the darkened room.

"Good evening, Chief," Savalas said coldly. He placed himself directly in front of the glass wall. He didn't want to miss anything, especially with Barthold Meane sitting there too.

"She's a suspect?"

Savalas was trying to follow the conversation between McGinnis and Maureen Dorsay, not Bartholdo's commentary.

"Yes, Sir. Main suspect."

"Anyone else in line?"

"Not sure yet, Sir. Gotta ask the detective about that."

Savalas dreaded it. Barthold Meane was not shutting up. Savalas didn't want to give away any leads without the detective's consent. He knew that McGinnis and Bartholdo had their differences, and he, Savalas, was not going to stand in the middle of them.

"Let's see what she got then," Bartholdo finally said.

*Thank God, this conversation is over*, Savalas thought.

***

"I didn't do it!" Maureen shouted.

"So you know what happened, Mrs. Dorsay. You don't mind if I call you Maureen, do you?"

"I didn't kill her, Mr. Ginnis!"

"McGinnis, please."

"Whatever, Detective. I want a lawyer."

"You will get a lawyer, Maureen, but one thing at a time. Would you mind explaining to me why you were not aboard that airplane to Arkansas with your husband? You did have a ticket, didn't you?"

"Yes Sir, I had a ticket. I told Alan months ago that I did not want to adopt a child as long as he was still drinking alcohol. He neither quit drinking nor gave up on the adoption. So my only way out of it was not to go on that plane!"

"Why were you talking about adopting a child, if I may ask? Are you unable to have children, Maureen?"

"That's what my husband thinks!"

"You told your husband you couldn't have children, even though you can?"

"It's like I told you, Mr. Ginnis, my husband is an alcoholic. He comes home drunk almost every other day now. There is no way I am having children with a drunk. Since Alan tends to have a shallow grasp on reality, I avoided conflict by telling him that I couldn't have any kids. I've been taking the pill for five years now. But then he came up with the idea to adopt a child."

"Interesting. You got a difficult situation there, Maureen. I have to admit that. But tell me–you have any side action?"

Maureen was getting angry. "That's none of your business Detective, and I repeat, I want a lawyer!"

"And I repeat, you will get your lawyer. Just answer this one last question, please. Where were you on the night that Mrs. Woodbridge got killed? You have any alibi?"

Maureen slammed her fist on the table, "I want my lawyer, now!"

"Okay, okay, Maureen. I see there is no talking to you. If you mind us, the lieutenant will escort you to your cell. If you refuse to talk to us, I'm afraid we are going to have to keep you in here until we can continue this discussion in the company of your lawyer tomorrow. Lieutenant!"

Savalas was already standing inside the interrogation room before McGinnis could say his name. He was just glad he didn't have Bartholdo staring a hole into his back. You never knew what that slimeball was thinking.

"And as for you, Maureen, I'm afraid to tell you that you'll remain in custody until you have evidence to prove that you were not at the crime scene that night. We have a piece of evidence found at the crime scene that suggests that the murderer had platinum blonde hair. You have platinum blond hair, Maureen. Ah, excuse me!" Almost unnoticed, McGinnis pulled a strand of blonde hair off of Maureen's navy blue work blazer.

"And that's for Dr. Pepperstone, our forensic specialist. Maybe with several strands in comparison, the analysis will be easier," McGinnis justified his unusual move.

For the first time, she stared at him with her mouth wide open. "Hey!"

Savalas escorted her out, and McGinnis walked into his office. Once everyone had left the interrogation room, Barthold Meane picked up his legs off of the desk and stood. He felt sure that this case would be closed before the week was over. As usual, McGinnis was doing excellent work. Barthold Meane sighed and left the observation room.

***

"I got another sample, Jack," explained the detective. "Can you take a look at it and compare it with what we found at the crime site? I will be conducting another interrogation with the suspect tomorrow morning."

He was sitting in his cubicle, talking to his old colleague Dr. Jack Pepperstone. Thanks to Dr. Pepperstone's scientific talents, he had solved many apparently hopeless cases.

"How many years have I known you now, Peter? Twenty-five? Do you always have to send me your samples at the last minute? I'm supposed to be home for dinner, and I'm already working overtime. I was not planning on skipping that dinner tonight."

McGinnis checked his wristwatch. It was a 7:45. Everyone else in the department left at 5:00. Jack was right. He had been working several hours overtime.

"We're carved from the same stone, Jack. I could also use some time off. So how about this? Maybe you can put it under the microscope first thing in the morning. I'm having it sent over to yourdepartment now."

A police officer came into McGinnis' office looking for the sample. The detective carefully placed the hair sample inside a plastic bag, labeled it as evidence, and dated it.

The officer, who was obviously new to his job, stood there, waiting for instruction. McGinnis just nodded and waved him away. He covered the phone receiver with his hand. "Take this to forensics. They will take care of it."

"Okay, Detective." The young officer left the room with the small bag of evidence.

McGinnis continued his conversation, "Thanks, Jack. I appreciate your hard work."

"Without me, you would be nowhere, Detective! You know that."

McGinnis sighed. The old forensics chief gave him this talk every time. There was no turning it off.

"Yes, I know, Jack. You're the real artist, here. A crime artist!"

"All right then, Peter. I'll look at it first thing tomorrow morning. Nothing much going on here anyway. Just old stuff. Good night, now. Promise me that you'll take *your* tired ass out of the office, too. There ain't no point in chasing crime when you're too tired to catch it!"

"I promise, Jack. Bye now. And hey, thanks, ol' pal!"

"Don't worry about it. That's what I'm here for."

McGinnis put down the receiver. It was good to know there were some people you could rely on, even if it was just a handful. His old colleague Dr. Pepperstone was one of them. Pepperstone had been working for the police even longer than he had. Pepperstone's retirement was only two years from now. McGinnis dreaded the moment when his old pal from the forensics department wouldn't be there anymore. There would be no one left he could trust in the whole building.

McGinnis sighed. He got up, picked up his newsboy hat from the coat rack, placed it on his semi-bald head, snapped off the light, and left his office. He checked the cubicle next door; the light was still on. That must be the lieutenant, typing up today's report.

The light of the computer screen was reflecting Savalas' handsome features. Otherwise, the room was dark.

"Sir? You should go home, Lieutenant. It's late."

"I know. Let me just finish this up."

"Thanks, Savalas. You're a good man."

"What's your plan for tomorrow, Detective?"

"We still gotta check the alibi of that son of Ray's."

"What's the location?"

"24-Hour Fitness on Colorado Blvd."

"Now, that sounds like my type of territory. You want me to go?" McGinnis considered. He knew that if there was something wrong with the alibi, they were going to have to bring in the Persian Adonis. And should he not cooperate, McGinnis's body was definitely not fit enough for wild crime chases, anymore.

"Yeah, why not? You go. Check in with me here when you have the information. I'll be conducting another interrogation with the Dorsay lady, as soon as I get the evidence in from the hair."

"Consider it done, McGinnis."

"All right, now. Don't stay too long. Good night, Lieutenant."

"Bye, now."

McGinnis left the lieutenant in the miniature office cubicle. As he left the building, he felt a glimpse of hope. *Maybe this one will stay*. He opened the door of his beat-up Ford Futura and started the motor.

***

The sun was gone, but McGinnis was restless. He didn't feel like going home just yet. It was only 8:30 PM. Nell was probably out doing something. She couldn't be bothered. Maybe he should check out the Lucky Baldwin's before going home, and see what old Tim Simmons had to say. Thinking about the future alcohol level in his blood, McGinnis first drove his car home and parked it under the designated carport on Parkwood Street. He didn't care about entering the modest walls of his apartment. He grabbed the key from the ignition of his old Ford Futura and walked to the Lucky Baldwin's. The walk through the still-warm evening air did him good.

***

"Howdy, Detective," Tim greeted him from behind the mahogany bar. McGinnis waved as he walked through the bar to the men's room. He exited the men's room and seated himself in a back booth. McGinnis avoided the entrance area like a disease. What he didn't see didn't concern him. He stuck to the back of the bar.

"Same as usual?" Tim came to his table to take his order.

"Yep. Same as usual."

Relieved, the detective took his newsboy hat off and carefully placed it on the table. He sighed, looking around the familiar bar. It was Wednesday, and the bar was somewhat busier than usual although it was still the off-season. He was sitting with his back to the entrance but could see the entire room in the reflection of the wall mirror, which was a huge advertisement for his favorite beer. McGinnis nearly bit off part of his upper lip when he saw the receptionist of Adon & Co. standing in the doorway. She was accompanied by some big-shot office geek. It was not Assim. *He must not be in the mood for partying right now*, McGinnis figured.

At first, the young lady didn't see him. Stunned by the coincidence, McGinnis kept staring at her.

His drink was waiting for him at the bar, but Tim would serve it to him soon. The carbon dioxide would rise to the top, creating the world-famous, irresistible, thick foam. Meanwhile, McGinnis studied the malicious receptionist.

She was very busy attempting to impress the good-looking businessman. *Cheap receptionist is trying to secure her future by wrapping a high-salaried lawyer around her finger*, McGinnis figured. The two giggled and chatted until the pretty Latina woman finally noticed McGinnis looking at her through the mirror. Her jaw dropped. She stood still for a moment, and the conversation stopped. The lawyer walked to the bar alone, unaware that his company had fallen behind. Self-conscious of how she had just given herself away, the young receptionist quickly caught up with her suitor as he turned, looking for her. Reflexively, she squeezed her body very close to his and made out with the man to hide her embarrassing exposure. Her companion didn't seem to mind at all.

McGinnis shrugged the ridiculous scene off with a short outburst of laughter. It stopped as quickly as it had come to him. Tim stood there with his drink. "Your stout is ready, Detective." Tim placed the large glass on a coaster.

"Thank you, pal," McGinnis said. Tim hurried away. He was the only waiter in the room, and people were waiting at the bar.

"Be back in a little," he gave McGinnis a heads-up. Tim always enjoyed hearing the newest news from the detective. McGinnis gave him a nod.

"No worries."

McGinnis took a small sip from his large drink. He hoped the people from the law office would go make out somewhere else. Beer didn't taste as good when consumed among the wrong company.

Sure enough, the young receptionist achieved her goal by snuggling up to her fancy suitor. She managed to convince him to hang out elsewhere. She mischievously guided the lawyer out of the bar. McGinnis was relieved. He could finally drink his beer in peace.

The bar was quiet again. "So what's new, Detective?" Tim joined the detective in his booth with a panaché, a popular French drink with little alcohol. "Found the culprit yet?"

"Not quite." McGinnis took another sip from his tall glass. It was half-empty by now. "But getting there. Probably done with this case by the end of the week."

"Did the writer's assistant get out?"

"Oh yeah. Her employer bailed her out before the night was over. Complete waste of money, by the way. The girl would have been free to go only one hour later. But then again, these entertainment people just don't seem to worry too much about expenses. But we already got a new blonde waiting in the cell."

"I thought Ray West was a writer?"

"His wife is an entertainment lawyer. She's the one who arranged all that."

"Interesting," Tim said and took a sip from his panaché. He couldn't afford to drink much alcohol when he was on duty. He wouldn't be able to account for the safekeeping of the place. Tim Simmons was a good guy. He was reliable and competent.

"Suspicious, no?"

"Yes, but Ray West didn't do it. I checked his alibi. What about his wife?"

"Hmm. Interesting question. I haven't thought about that. Female, middle-aged entertainment lawyer kills Jewish senior citizen. Why? Jealousy?"

McGinnis snickered. "You're funny."

"To finally cash in on that rent money that the old lady was not paying? They gave the lady's home to the writer, right? I remember you telling me that, I think." Tim Simmons was on track. He had a good nose for crime. No wonder he was studying criminology.

"Yes, that's a theory. But I have to disappoint you. Our investigations are currently leading us in another direction. The lady from the backhouse is not telling us something. And the alibi of the property manager, who had access to all the houses, is currently being checked."

"Oh, well. Good luck with that," Tim said, disappointed that his ideas weren't going to be used. He finished his drink.

"How's your writing coming along?" the detective asked, hoping to cheer him up.

"Oh that, yes. I'm creating a family drama where the head of the family gets murdered by intoxication to manipulate the order of the inheritance."

"Sounds interesting. Let me give you a word of advice, ol' pal. You're a smart boy. I know you're studying hard to go into crime investigation. But this business is not good for a positive, young soul like yours. No matter how tough you think you are, looking at all those crime scenes all the time messes with your head. Look at me. My mind is filled with criminals and corpses, constantly putting together the missing pieces of these endless puzzles. Even when I'm not working, my mind continues to go back to these horrible images. It's torture. I'm almost incapable of thinking anything pleasant these days. You don't want to get this way. If you want to take a word of advice from someone who knows, finish your degree, finish your book, publish your book, and then be free to do something positive with your life!" McGinnis swallowed the remaining half of his tall glass in one gulp and got up.

Tim stared at him, fascinated. "Thank you, Detective. I'll keep that in mind," Tim Simmons said. He took the empty glasses to the bar.

Exhausted, Detective McGinnis walked to the door and gave Tim Simmons a salute with a tip of his hat. "Good night now, ol' pal." The glass door of the Irish Pub swung open, and the detective was gone.

Tim Simmons walked back to the table where he'd been sitting with the detective. McGinnis was a true find. He felt like wrapping up right away and going to his desk to work on his book, but he couldn't. He was in charge of the bar tonight. He gave the table a quick swipe with the dishcloth and picked up the large tip that the detective had left for him. Tim walked back to the bar, which was empty by now. He hoped no one else would come in, so he could close up early.

# Pursuing a Maroon Infinity

The next morning, Peter McGinnis took his time. He knew that Savalas would have a while to wait for the alibi to be verified, and the lawyer Maureen had requested would not be there before eleven. Twenty-five years of practice had taught him about people and their habits, and he knew that lawyers were always late.

Therefore, he decided to stop by the cafe to see if Nell was there.

***

"Howdy!"

"Howdy, Detective. Long time no see." A long stare was exchanged, the kind of lingering look that two people who cared about each other share, especially if they haven't talked in a long time.

McGinnis looked down in shame.

"Been busy, huh?" Nell, a weathered beauty with ginger colored hair, looked straight at him. McGinnis, who was usually the first to open up his mouth, just nodded in silence. Nell smiled.

"Coffee?"

McGinnis grinned from ear to ear. He could be grumpy like the Grinch himself, but when you got a smile out of the detective, it was infectious.

"And a bagel, please. Toasted, with cream cheese."

"Hungry, huh?"

McGinnis nodded again.

"You eating that here or taking it out?" Nell asked.

"Eating here!" McGinnis quickly replied.

"Wow!" Nell was surprised. McGinnis never stayed. He never had time. Today, he was almost throwing it at her.

"You on vacation or something, Peter?" Nell asked as she handed him the coffee cup.

"Nope. Just waitin' for the lawyer."

"Oh, I see. Well, it's nice you came in here on your morning off."

"No excuse too small, to take a look at your beautiful face," the detective flirted.

*Wow, he must be having a good day*, Nell thought. *Since he's in such a good mood, now is the time to ask him out.*

"What are you doing this weekend, Peter? You wanna go for a little hike through the mountains with me?" Nell asked.

The bagel was ready, and she took it promptly to the table where McGinnis was sitting. She sat down with him. She devoured him with her eyes as he was clumsily piling the cream cheese on the first half. Nell had put additional portions on his plate because she was well aware of the detective's eating habits.

McGinnis knew she was looking at him, but he pretended to be busy with his breakfast. Her gaze was making him a bit nervous. He would have never admitted it.

"I don't know yet. Probably, if it goes like I think it will, I'm free. The case is looking good. But you never know, in my line of business."

He took a huge bite from this delicious piece of culinary artwork, leaving a white blob of cheese in the corner of his mouth. The morning was always the busiest time at her shop, and Nell had to get back behind the counter. People kept pouring through the door. She got up and wiped the corner of the detective's mouth clean with the tip of her thumb. Before McGinnis could protest, the spot was gone.

"Call me if you have time. I'm going on the Mount Wilson Trail. You can meet me in the Sierra Madre town center."

McGinnis tried to say something, but his mouth was full of bagel. He just nodded. Nell smiled. That was her detective. She admired him. He was an adult on the outside, and a clumsy child on the inside. *Too bad he always has so much to do.*

McGinnis' pager was beeping. *Oh-oh. Trouble at the gym.*

He dropped the other half of the bagel, grabbed his coffee, and left in a rush.

"I'll give you a call if I have time, Nell!"

"Okay. And stay out of trouble, Detective!"

A worried Nell watched McGinnis race out of her shop, spilling coffee all over his shirt in the process. *That man so needs a woman in his life*, she thought.

***

Savalas drove to police headquarters and changed cars. He had been up since five in the morning, working out at the very same gym where he was supposed to check the alibi. He wanted to be all rigged out on an official mission like this, because you never knew when you might need it. He decided to wait a while on the investigation, and return to the location at official working hours.

At precisely 8:30 in the morning, Savalas stepped out of his police cruiser on Oakland Avenue, right in front of Le Cordon Bleu cooking school. As a member of this gym, he was quite familiar with the surroundings. He had always found it an interesting combination, having a gym situated right next to a cooking school. *You can burn off all those calories right after you create them*, he figured. Amused, he walked to the back door of the old Art Deco construction and entered the building.

A large stairway led him to the reception desk of the underground facility, where an argument between a client and an employee was in full swing. Savalas couldn't see the client's face, but he was huge, and dressed all in black. He could see that the manager, a petite brunette in her early twenties, was being threatened. "If you don't change it, I will cancel my membership, and I will have you fired!" the muscle man said.

"It's like I already told you. I can't change what's stored in the system. Once the time clock has you registered, that's what gets saved. If you want to change the system, you have to find an IT guy to do that or something, and I'm not sure that's legal."

"I'm sure there is a way to access the time clock registry! You're just too fucking stupid to do that! Who's your manager? I want to speak to the local branch manager right now!" The unfriendly male continued his verbal abuse.

"Mr. Esfahani?"

Even though he was officially on another mission, Lieutenant Savalas knew that he needed to intervene. He hoped that this coincidence wouldn't interfere with his plans to verify the alibi.

The unfriendly male turned around. Yes indeed, it was Assim Esfahani. Savalas' mind worked fast. On one hand, he didn't want to mess up his mission, because he still didn't know whether the suspect's alibi was real. On the other hand, it was his duty as an officer to stop this man from threatening the girl at the reception.

"Stop threatening that girl," Savalas ordered simply. *It's good when you can take recourse to the power of your uniform when you don't necessarily feel the authority within yourself,* Savalas thought with relief. Especially when dealing with a bully the size of Assim and after working out on the treadmill for over 45 minutes earlier. Savalas was exhausted.

"What do you want, officer? I'm not threatening anyone. How did you know my name, anyhow?"

The tall male's brain started to operate quickly. Assim stared into Savalas' face as if he had seen a ghost. Savalas had his right hand near his belt, ready to arrest the abusive customer at any moment.

Before Savalas could answer, Assim pushed him to the side and escaped through the steep stairway, taking three stairs at a time. By the time Savalas got up, Assim was already at the door. *Damn! He's getting away!* Savalas followed him up the stairs. He dialed McGinnis' private cell number on the way. "Alibi verification failed. Suspect is escaping!"

"Go get him!" McGinnis ordered. "I'll verify the alibi."

Outside, Lieutenant Savalas saw a maroon Infinity shoot left onto Union Street. That wasn't too bad; they were right around the corner from headquarters. The trick was to keep him close.

Savalas threw on his seatbelt and stepped on the gas pedal. He was able to see the Infinity cut around another corner, at Los Robles. The suspect was trying to get out of sight. He would probably try to get on the freeway. The Infinity had to be stopped from entering the freeway under any circumstances!

Savalas contacted traffic control. He wanted a traffic blockade in front of the freeway entrance at Colorado Boulevard, *now*.

"Yes. The suspect's car is a maroon Infinity, personalized California license number reads ASSIM 1. The car must be stopped, under all circumstances!"

Savalas listened to the dispatcher ordering units to block off the freeway access. Meanwhile, Assim had turned right onto Corson. He was headed toward Lake Street. *The man must be nervous*, Savalas thought. He was leading Savalas around the Civic District. This was Savalas' territory; no way was he letting Assim get away, not in *his* territory.

On Lake Street, the Infinity skipped a red light and turned right, back into Walnut. Savalas stomped on the gas. He was right behind Assim now. Savalas made an announcement with his loudspeaker. "Pull over to the right and stop, *now!*"

Suddenly, right in front of headquarters, the Infinity turned left. *What's he trying to do? Deliver himself to the police?* No, he sped on past.

At the circle in front of City Hall, Assim made a full U-Turn and headed north, toward Walnut, but then he turned right into Ramona Street. Savalas tried to cut him off at the intersection, but there was a woman with a baby carriage in the crosswalk, so he had to stop.

*Better not go north, or I'll catch you at the end of Euclid,* Savalas thought. The Infinity turned right and sped onto Colorado. There he was, heading straight toward the freeway. The Infinity ran several red lights. Savalas had a hard time keeping up with him. He was trying not to run over the pedestrians crossing the street at Fair Oaks Avenue. Savalas made another announcement with his loudspeaker. "Slow down and pull over to the right!" The Infinity continued to risk lives, speeding over the bridge past St. John Street. *Does he not see that a barricade is waiting for him right after the Norton Simmons Museum?* He tried to make a U-turn and escaped the blockade, but Savalas had stopped his vehicle at a ninety-degree angle to the traffic. He jumped out of the car and pointed his firearm at the Infinity. The driver of the Infinity was in serious trouble now. He was prepared to threaten the driver with a gunshot. It was clear the Infinity was out of options. It came to a full stop.

"Mr. Esfahani. Step out of your vehicle, now!"

Assim slowly stepped out of his car. The lieutenant grabbed his arm, pushed him against his car, and handcuffed his hands behind his back.

"You have nothing on me. I have an alibi!" Assim protested.

"We will just see about that. Meanwhile, you are coming with me for obstruction of justice and a full series of traffic violations."

Savalas didn't hesitate. He pulled the tall man away from his car and pushed him into the back of his police car.

"Watch your head!" He warned Assim, who still almost hit his head getting inside the vehicle. Savalas pushed his head down at the last second, and closed the door firmly. *That* one was done for a while.

# Cross-Interrogation

"Sit down and wait!" Lieutenant Savalas ordered. He'd decided it was best to have Assim wait in the interrogation room, because that's where McGinnis would want to have him when he talked to him.

Savalas knew that McGinnis would be there any minute. Frankly, he didn't care if the suspect had to wait. It served him right.

"The detective will be asking you some questions."

"I want a lawyer!" Assim protested, but Savalas had already slammed the door shut. He was fed up with the bully who had unnecessarily risked hundreds of pedestrians' lives.

***

McGinnis came into the police station panting for breath. After the experience at the gym, he decided that he could use some exercise and took the stairs. The result was an embarrassment. If anyone needed a gym membership, it was him, and he knew it. But he refused to participate in that competition of physical abilities and muscle pumping. *Gym people are show-offs.* Fortunately, Savalas came walking down the hallway. *Finally!*

"Oh, here you are, McGinnis! The suspect's waiting for you in the interrogation room. Did you get the evidence?"

McGinnis waved the folder in Savalas' face. It gave him a cool breeze in this sticky hallway of Police Headquarters. "Yep. Tell me now. What happened?"

"I ran into him at the gym when he was trying to threaten an employee into changing his check-in hours. When I interrupted him, he ran off. I chased his car all through Old Town."

"How did you catch him?"

"We blocked off the freeway. Figured he'd try to get on from Colorado. And that's exactly what he did. When he couldn't go any further, I forced him out of his car. So here he is."

They walked back up the hallway and peeked through the window of the observation room, into the room where the suspect was sitting. Assim sat there and stared into the void, as if nothing had happened.

"Strange dude," McGinnis said.

"Anything from the other suspect's lawyer?"

"Yes, Sir. She said she was coming. Should be here any minute now."

"I have an idea," McGinnis said as he walked out of the observation room, turning toward the interrogation room.

"Cross-interrogation?" Savalas guessed.

He just watched McGinnis' head going up and down and a finger tipping his hat, confirming the thought, as he hurried down the hallway.

"Gotcha," Savalas said has he took a place in front of the window. He was going to watch from the outside and not budge. The detective thought that he had everything under control, but you never knew, with a bully like that in interrogation. McGinnis was not the youngest anymore, and frankly, not the fittest. Of course, those were things that Savalas would never tell him directly. But he could stay there for safety, backup, and he didn't have any other orders for now.

***

"Good morning, Mr. Esfahani. It is still morning, isn't it?" McGinnis walked across the room toward the suspect, who was sitting there, confused.

"You don't mind, do you?" McGinnis picked up Assim's left arm and looked at the Rolex on his wrist. It was already 12:30. It was only because of his visit at Nell's Café that he didn't declare this morning wasted.

"Nice watch!" McGinnis stated. He was in a rather good mood, for once. "Where did you get it?" McGinnis asked.

Now Assim was even more confused. "I bought it, why? What does this have to do with why I'm sitting here? I want a lawyer!"

"It's an original, isn't it? And originals are expensive," McGinnis said bluntly.

"I make a good living," Assim answered. "I can afford it."

"I see that. Nothing goes over better than the American way, does it?"

"What do you want from me, Detective? I already told you everything I know about the case," Assim protested.

McGinnis started to pace the room. "You're in trouble, Mr. Esfahani. You broke pretty much every traffic rule there is, and besides all those violations, your alibi is false."

McGinnis started to look through the papers Kevin had printed for him. "It says here that you were at the gym from eight 'til ten PM, which still gives you plenty of time to have committed the crime. You do not have an alibi, Mr. Esfahani. You'd better come out with the truth!"

"I'm not a murderer, Mr. McGinnis," Assim said in his most charming voice. "Besides, I am not saying one more word until I get a lawyer."

"Sure. I'll take care of that. Meanwhile, please wait in here 'til I take care of your other matter."

"You have no right!" Assim protested.

"I do so," McGinnis shut him down, and quickly left the room.

"I want to get out of here!" Assim slammed his fist on the table, but McGinnis had already left the room. Savalas came to catch him in the hallway.

"Get the other suspect, quickly!" McGinnis ordered.

*Oh no, not that one*, Savalas thought as he rushed to the jail wing. "She won't budge without the presence of a lawyer."

"Tell her the lawyer is on her way, and we'll have her meet her in the interrogation room."

"Consider it done!" Savalas knew he had his hands full, again.

***

Savalas dragged Maureen through the hallway. He briefly stopped in front of McGinnis' office; he was on the phone getting Assim's lawyer. No need to wait for a state-assigned lawyer here. Assim had his own, so this was going to go faster.

McGinnis signaled for another officer to help Savalas bring the suspect into the interrogation room. He then waved them off.

The second officer unlocked the door, and Savalas brought Maureen to the other end of the table. He tried to watch Assim's face. It appeared that Assim's face twitched for a fraction of a second.

Maureen sat down. When she saw Assim, her expression froze. McGinnis was watching all this through the window of the observation room. Not a word was spoken. Then, out of nowhere, Assim screamed, "Where's my lawyer?"

"Coming!" McGinnis answered joyfully as he walked through the door of the interrogation room, accompanied by the two lawyers. The first one, Aileen McKinsley, was a blonde in a conservative blue skirt, carrying an attaché case. The second lawyer was a middle-aged Persian who looked like he'd seen a lot over the years, Dr. Elias Fahrad.

The detective watched the two suspects' faces intently. Their faces were locked, expressions frozen. "I love it when cases get solved easily," McGinnis said with a smile.

Assim's perfectly styled left eyebrow rose. The expression of panic came over Maureen's face.

"I didn't do it!" she said, and started to sob.

"Tissue?" Savalas offered. She took it resentfully.

"So, while we're waiting for your representatives to get settled, would you kindly let me know if you two know each other?"

"He's the property manager," Maureen sighed hopelessly.

"I am not saying one word without a consultation with Dr. Fahrad!" Assim continued to protest.

Right on cue, the lawyers asked for a moment to speak with their clients. They were escorted to a private room.

"So, what do you think?" McGinnis asked Savalas, as he paced up and down the interrogation room. Savalas was confused.

"What do I think? I don't know what I think! What do you mean?"

"Do the suspects know each other? In order to find a conclusion in this situation, it would be helpful to know if the suspects are in any kind of relationship with each other."

"You mean sexually?"

McGinnis nodded quietly, with a nasty grin on his face. The suspects walked back in. Savalas kept quiet and guarded the door.

"Welcome back, everybody. Please have a seat. You two on that end, and you two on that end."

Assim and Maureen were instructed to sit on opposite sides.

"So, would anyone mind answering my question now? Do you know each other?"

Maureen patiently nodded while Aileen answered for her. “My client says that she knows him as being the property manager, whom she pays rent to.”

“Do you confirm that?” McGinnis asked Dr. Fahrad.

“Yes, Detective. Mr. Esfahani manages all the tenants’ issues on Mr. West’s properties.”

“Does he receive the checks personally, or is there a place where the tenants can put them?” McGinnis wanted to know.

Assim whispered something into Fahrad’s ear. “Yes, Detective. There is a box attached to the side of Mr. West’s gate, where all the tenants can place their rent payments. Mr. Esfahani picks them up once per month, or whenever they are placed there.”

“Mr. Esfahani, are you personally acquainted with Mrs. Dorsay? Are all your relationships with the tenants at Ray’s property strictly reduced to the management of rent checks?”

“All of my client relationships at the property are strictly professional, and related to the management of the property only,” Elias answered for Assim again. McGinnis turned around.

“Mrs. Dorsay, are you in a sexual relationship with the suspect?” Maureen’s jaw dropped, and she helplessly looked at Aileen for assistance; she started to answer for her client.

“No, Mrs. McKinsley, I would like the suspect to answer the question for herself,” McGinnis insisted.

“Mrs. Dorsay, I am asking you again. Seeing that you are obviously not very happy with your current relationship, are you seeing someone else?”

Maureen looked around the room, hopelessly looking for help. She was all on her own. Assim kept staring at her angrily. Suddenly, she started to cry again.

“Yes, Detective. Mr. Esfahani and I have been seeing each other for the past month or so.” Savalas had to go and get a tissue. “But I didn’t kill Natalie. I’ve lived here for twelve years. I could never do such a thing. If you’re looking for the murderer, ask someone else!” She looked at Assim.

“We’ll get to that later. That’s all I needed to know, for now. We have to see what the forensics report shows about the mysterious hair strand.”

Assim snickered nastily. “Suspects dismissed!”

“I want to go home!” Maureen protested.

"You are not free to go just yet. If you wanted to be set on free foot, you should have shown a little bit more cooperation on the first day that we asked to speak to you. Or find someone to pay your bail!"

Assim snickered again.

"Stop it, asshole! You killed her! I *know* you killed her! Isaw you!" Maureen started screaming. Assim just continued to snicker. Aileen was trying to get her to stop talking, but she didn't have a chance. The words had already spilled.

"Escort her out!" McGinnis ordered. The other officer walked Maureen out of the room, followed by the lawyer. "I'll get back to you."

The door closed with a vehement shutter.

"And you! I won't ask you this again. What were you doing on Sunday night between eleven PM and one AM, Mr. Esfahani?"

Assim kept up the attitude. "Like I told you, Detective. I was at the gym!" Assim snickered again. McGinnis went through his papers again and handed Elias a copy.

"If you were at the gym from eight 'til ten PM that night, you still had plenty of time to do it. Where did you go after the gym? What did you do?"

Assim snickered again. "I don't know; I went home."

"Do you have any witnesses?"

Assim took a moment to think. "Ask Anselm. He'll confirm that. He lives at my place!"

McGinnis and Savalas exchanged a glance. Not a piece of information to be had out of this guy. They were going to have to do the inquiry all over again.

"All right, wise guy. We will find your friend and see what he has to say about all this. But meanwhile, you stay here!"

"Detective, seeing the lack of proof that you have, my client would like to request the payment of the bail for the traffic violations until more information comes to light in the case," Elias said.

"Damn him! He can go where he wants, but he'd better stay in town until this case is cleared," McGinnis yelled.

Savalas opened Assim's handcuffs, and he was free to go. Dr. Elias Fahrad escorted him out.

"I'll see you again!" McGinnis yelled after him. Assim just snickered.

"God damn it! Where is that forensics report?" McGinnis cursed, and smashed his fist on the table.

"Take it easy, Detective. That man is not going far. With the record that he just created for himself this morning, he's grounded for a while."

"That's what you think. These people with all the money, they always manage to work themselves out of these situations, especially if it's only traffic violations. We need to get more evidence. The way this case is going, we're gonna be nowhere at the end of this week, and you know how Bartholdo gets."

Savalas agreed. Something had to give.

# Turning in Circles

The next day, McGinnis was sitting in his office, thinking. *Why is it that the wise guy always gets set free?* Well, nothing was certain but he sure as hell wasn't going to let that liar get away that easily. The detective picked up the phone.

"Well hello there, Detective. Long time no speak."

"You got anything for me, Jack? Any fingerprints on the murder weapon?"

"Not a single print or shred of evidence on the menorah. The killer worked clean."

"What about the hair strand?"

"Looks better there. Even though the peroxide ruined most of it, I was able to find some traces of DNA, which resemble the one of the new strands you gave me yesterday."

"Really? Oh, damn that blonde!"

"What, you're not happy you finally got some evidence?"

McGinnis seriously considered the question. "Well, yes and no. I still got a wise guy running around free and the way this case is going, he's going to stay free, especially if he comes up with the money he owes for bail and traffic violations. And it looks like he's going to. He's a pretty successful candidate."

"Well, the killer is the killer. You wouldn't want an innocent person sitting in prison for the crimes of the culprit, would you?"

McGinnis shook his head. "Absolutely not. Which reminds me, I got work to do. Thank you, Jack. You got any plans for the weekend?"

"Checking out a new restaurant in Sierra Madre. La Cucina Del Diavolo, the Devil's Kitchen, an Italian restaurant. Everyone's talking about it. Just opened last week."

"Provocative name," McGinnis noted. "I hope the food tastes as good as the name sounds."

"We'll see about that. I'll give you a report about the restaurant Monday. Meanwhile, good luck with your case! Bye, now."

"Thanks, ol' pal. Bye, now. And regards to Lydia."

***

McGinnis hung up the phone. Then he picked it up again, and dialed Savalas on intercom.

"Savalas speaking."

"Come over to my office. I need you to find someone."

Less than half a minute later, Savalas was standing in McGinnis' artificially lit cubicle. The man desperately needed a change of scenery, and some fresh air.

"Who's that?" Savalas asked.

"Anselm Rodriguez. Mr. Esfahani's assistant. I'm wondering what he saw on Sunday night."

"What about the hair? Did Dr. Pepperstone find anything yet?"

"Yep. The strand that was found in Mrs. Woodbridge's house is Maureen's hair. It does not yet prove that she actually committed the crime, but it sure makes her our number one suspect."

"So you want me to track Anselm Rodrigues down and bring him here?"

"Yes, Lieutenant. That would definitely be a good thing."

"Where's the house, or is he going to be at work?"

"Not sure where he is right now. He could be at home or at work."

"Where's the work location?"

"At Assim's office. The office building on Corson Street."

"You want me to see if I can find him there first?"

"Yes, Savalas. Go there first!"

***

Two minutes later, Savalas was in his police car, heading west toward the building containing Assim's office. He hoped he wouldn't have to stop traffic again to catch *this* witness. One car chase a week was enough.

He parallel parked his car on Townsend Street and walked to the lobby. Savalas enjoyed the calm of the beautifully landscaped courtyard. Contrary to the detective's aesthetic sense, he was able to appreciate the improvements in lifestyle that modernity had brought.

He carefully opened the glass door to the lobby and approached the receptionist. "Where's Adon and Company?" he asked.

"Third floor," the heavyset Asian receptionist said. "Elevators are right there."

"Thank you!"

Savalas walked to the elevator and carefully observed the elegant entry hall. It was made out of the type of luxury materials that he would never have. In his culture, marble floors and golden doorknobs existed, but they were usually the result of some form of corruption. The debacle in Greece was proof enough of how corruption influenced some of the financial decisions made back in his home culture. His aversion to the flow of business procedures had been the motivation for him to join the police. He wanted to distinguish himself from the questionable reputation his ancestors had left him with.

*Ding*! The elevator arrived at the third floor. Adon & Co. The big logo above the entryway glimmered gold in the light from large, plate-glass windows. The same Latina secretary was guarding the phone lines. Her pretty jaw dropped a little when she saw a cop walk in again, a second time in just one week. She was on the phone, playing busy.

Savalas didn't waste any time. He showed her his license. "I'm looking for Anselm Rodriguez," he told her, while she was still on the phone.

She looked at this license, then at him. "Just a moment!" she insisted.

The pretty Latina hung up the phone.

"How can I help you?" She pretended she hadn't heard his initial request.

"I'm looking for Anselm Rodriguez," he said again.

Nervous, she went back to the phone. When Anselm picked up, she turned her back to Savalas and whispered, "There's another cop here. He's looking for *you* now."

"Hey, thanks. I'm out of here!" he replied.

Now she turned to Savalas, still with the phone in her hand.

"All right then, goodbye," she said, and hung up.

"Mr. Rodriguez will be here shortly to walk you to his office."

Savalas hesitated. He looked at the couch and decided he didn't have time for waiting.

"You take me to his office *now*!" He hated when he had to enforce things. The young Latina looked at him with big, helpless hazel eyes.

"But he said he would be right here..."

"I said take me there! Now!"

Out of options, the Latina stepped out of her safe zone behind the reception desk and started walking Savalas through the labyrinth of office cubicles and unused law books.

They were just about to turn a corner when Savalas heard a door slam shut.

"What was that?" he asked.

"I don't know," the Latina lied.

When they came around the corner, Savalas saw the door to an emergency exit.

"An exit! Hey, is he trying to get away?"

The Latina said nothing.

Savalas opened the door to the emergency exit and heard heavy footsteps running downwards.

"Mr. Rodriguez, this is the police. Stop right now!"

The footsteps continued. *Damn! He's getting away!*

"And as for you miss, you will hear from us for obstruction of justice!" Savalas screamed at the Latina secretary as she hurried back to her reception desk, her safe zone.

***

Savalas chased him down the stairs. The door slammed shut. *Damn*! Here he was again, chasing a suspect, while McGinnis was comfortably figuring out things from his desk at the office. Why didn't these people just wait? He would catch them anyway, it was just a matter of time. The charges would be lesser if they didn't run. *Oh well! Adolescents! They're young and stupid.* Rodriguez was not a full adult yet; he was seventeen years old. *Who knows how he got involved in this?*

Savalas exited, looking to the left and right. There was no suspect in sight. There were no pedestrians in sight to give him a hint. He checked the name of the street. Summit Avenue. Yes, the emergency exit had taken him to the west side of the building. Not a chance to catch up with the suspect, when his car was parked on Townsend.

There it came. The white Nissan Sentra sped across Walnut Street, heading east. Savalas caught a glimpse of the driver. The driver had long brown hair and glasses. It was Rodriguez.

Savalas dialed the office.

"Any luck?" the familiar voice asked.

"Suspect's escaping again. Heading east on Walnut."

"Uh, oh. I think I know where he's heading."

"Where's that?"

"Try his parents' house. Packing his belongings and leaving town 'til things cool down, I imagine."

Savalas wondered how McGinnis had figured this out again. But right now, he didn't have time to think.

"What's the address? Maybe I can catch him there."

"That would be great, since the young man is currently our only lead in this case. I was hoping to solve this case by Friday and go hiking with Nell. It's already Thursday, and things aren't looking so good."

"The address..?" Savalas had no time for smart talk.

"Wait a minute." Savalas could just see the detective scrolling through his iPhone as if he'd never seen a modern display in his life.

"Hurry! The witness is escaping!"

"Got it; I got it here. East Pasadena, 35 Backus Avenue."

"Thanks, Detective. Heading there ASAP."

"Let me know if you need backup."

"I think I can handle a seventeen-year-old."

"Good luck!"

***

Savalas hurried to his vehicle parked on Townsend. Jumping in, he flipped on the sirens and raced via Colorado Blvd. East toward the address. He eventually lowered his speed when he turned onto Del Mar Avenue. Traffic was lighter there, and it was markedly less dangerous to skip a red light on Del Mar than it was on Colorado, with all the pedestrians. Also, the witness was probably heading down Colorado; given the heavy traffic on that main road of Pasadena, Savalas might get there faster, or at least without too much delay.

When he finally reached Backus Street and saw the shabby-looking houses, he remembered where he was. This was the back road of the DMV. Everyone who lived in Pasadena had passed this road at some point, and it was as though the houses suffered from the frequency of the anonymous passers-by. Most of them were either run down or had a considerable amount of junk stacked up in the yard, as if to build a wall against the subtle daily intrusions.

As he counted down the house numbers, Savalas slowed the pace of his vehicle so he wouldn't attract attention. There were almost certainly police cars on this street every day.

There it was! Thirty-five Backus Street was a little green Spanish-style house, tiny actually, probably a one-bedroom, or maybe two very small ones. Its dried, brown yard was protected by an iron fence. The palm trees cast shade over the entrance.

Savalas drove all the way up to Backus Street. He made a U-turn at the Thurston Screen shop. He double-parked. He didn't want to risk losing the witness again because his car was parked too far away, and the other Backus Street parking spots were taken by people who couldn't find a space in the DMV lot.

He grabbed his license and approached the picturesque house. The front door was slightly ajar. He knocked; this caused the door to open slightly more.

A middle-aged Mexican woman in a traditional dress approached the door. Savalas heard rustling in the back. The lady turned back to the room from where the rustling was coming and yelled, "Anselmo! Qué acontece? Está la policía!"

The rustling stopped. Then, Savalas heard some squeaking and a thump.

"Soy Lieutenant Savalas, de la Policía de Pasadena. Estoy buscando Anselm Rodruiguez. Hay una ventana qué abre en el jardín?" He asked the old lady, in broken Spanish.

The lady looked at him as though he were Chinese. "Sí, hay," she muttered.

Savalas stuck his badge back into his shirt and ran around the house into the parking lot. He could see Anselm getting away through the garden of the backhouse. *Damn! Not another escape. What kind of week is this, anyway?* They had him chasing suspects around like he was racing in a marathon.

He started to run and called out, "Mr. Rodriguez, I advise you to stop. Running won't help you. We will catch you, no matter what, and whether you escape today or not! We just want to ask you a few questions."

The runner with the bag and the long hair slowed down. Savalas caught up with him and was about to isolate him on the ground when the witness finally spoke.

"Stop! Don't do that," Anselmo shouted. "I will come with you. My parents already saw you, so it doesn't matter anymore. Just don't put me in handcuffs. My mother would get too upset if she saw that."

"All right, Anselm. You're not an official suspect, so I'll make an exception. I'll just escort you to the car by the arm, but you'd better not try to run."

"I won't," Anselm promised.

Savalas escorted him through the driveway, and into the back of his car. Thank goodness, this hadn't gone too badly.

# New Roads

It was not necessary to drag the witness into headquarters. He seemed to be cooperative. Given Savalas' experiences from this week, he didn't want to take any unnecessary risks. He was extra careful to be sure that Anselm didn't run away.

"You don't have to pull my arm like that, Lieutenant; I can walk by myself," Anselm complained.

"Just making sure you don't play any more games, I've truly had enough for a while." Savalas justified his stronghold as he walked Anselm through the hallway of the police station.

McGinnis came along the hallway and met the two struggling men.

"Hey, hey, hey, Lieutenant. I don't think that'll be necessary. This young man isn't going anywhere, is he?" McGinnis advised the over-worked lieutenant, looking pointedly at Anselm.

Anselm shook his head. "No, I'm not!"

"I got him." In a fatherly gesture, McGinnis put his arm around the young witness and walked him to the interrogation room.

McGinnis opened the door, and Anselm sat down. He didn't seem intimidated at all.

"Want some coffee, or water?" McGinnis tried to lighten up the atmosphere.

"No thanks." Anselm didn't want to be stuck there any longer than necessary, so he turned down anything that might prolong his stay.

"We only have a few questions regarding your employer. We are still trying to verify that alibi, as I believe you've already heard us say. Assim mentioned something about your being able to verify his actions on Sunday night when I came over to your office the other day, remember?"

Unable to deny his relations with Assim, Anselm simply spoke the truth.

"He lets me stay at his place during the week, and I work with him in his office, so I kind of know what he's up to, most of the time."

Savalas entered the interrogation room and stood guard, just to be sure. He didn't trust anyone in this case anymore. McGinnis advised him to get a glass of water for the witness, no matter what Anselm's response had been. Savalas nodded and left the room.

McGinnis patiently waited. Silence filled the room. Savalas came back with a glass of water and put it in front of Anselm.

"Thank you!" Anselm said and took a sip.

*What a well-mannered young man,* McGinnis thought. *He says 'thank you' like a gentleman during a police investigation. What a shame that he has such nasty friends.*

"I know all this must be hard for you. Mr. Esfahani probably takes good care of you, doesn't he?"

"He's a good boss. Very generous with commissions. He shows me the business."

"How did you meet Mr. Esfahani, Anselm, if I may ask?"

"At the gym."

McGinnis and Savalas exchanged a glance. *Of course! It was at that gym!*

"I was trying the weights when Assim came in and showed me how to pick them up without hurting my back. He's very experienced at weights," Anselm explained.

"I know. Go on," McGinnis said.

"When I thanked him for the tip, he asked me what I did for a living, if I was going to school or anything. I told him that I was taking some classes in finance and administration at the community college."

"I see. Go on," McGinnis encouraged.

"He then told me that he was an independent real estate broker, and he needed an assistant. He told me that he could only pay me minimum wage, but if I sold something, I'd get the commission. I was actually thinking about going into real estate when I was done with college, so I couldn't believe how this opportunity just came to me out of nowhere. I accepted the offer immediately, and came to work at his office the next day. I've been working for Assim ever since. I've earned considerable amounts of money through the deals that he was able to make through me. He even lets me stay at his house when I don't feel like sleeping at my parents' house. He's very cool that way."

"I see," McGinnis frowned. "He's been good to you that way. Do your parents ever wonder where you are when you don't come home at night?"

Anselm took another sip of water. "I told them that I stay at Assim's house. They don't like it very much, but they also don't seem to really mind. I've been helping them with their mortgage ever since I got that job."

McGinnis started to chew on his upper lip. He was deep in thought. "You do realize that Mr. Esfahani is one of the principal suspects in a homicide case we're investigating?"

Slowly, Anselm looked down and nodded: "Yes."

"Now, there's something I would really like to know."

McGinnis made sure he had eye contact with his witness. "Has Mr. Esfahani ever made any anti-Semitic remarks in your presence?"

Savalas was quite surprised to hear that question, but then again, that was McGinnis. He was always prepared with something unexpected. It was probably the reason he was so successful in the homicide division.

The question seemed to strike a chord. At least, Anselm wasn't as talkative as he was before.

"Has Mr. Esfahani ever made any anti-Semitic remarks?" McGinnis repeated the question.

Silently, and slowly, Anselm's head began to nod, "Yes Sir, a lot."

"And has he ever made any remarks about the old lady who lives for free on his father's property?"

Ashamed, Anselm looked down, "Yes, he has."

"What kind of remarks?" McGinnis wanted to know.

Anselm thought for a moment, remembering, and then replied, "He said something about Jewish people all being the same, because they had too much money, and that the only good Jew was a dead Jew, because there was usually some money to be got out of them."

"Wow!" McGinnis took a step back.

That was too much, even for a tough guy like him. *What a thing to say!* He took his hat off and scratched his head, then put it back on again. "This is just between the two of us; nobody's going to pin you down on anything you say here. But I'd like to know, do you think it's possible that Assim killed that lady?"

Terrified, Anselm looked down again. He didn't answer. McGinnis waited 'til he had eye contact again. He leaned on the table and looked the young man straight in the eye.

"Do you think it's possible?"

Anselm held his gaze for several seconds, and then he looked down again. He whispered, "I guess it could be possible."

That's what McGinnis wanted to hear. Relieved, he got up and paced the room. He exchanged a glance with Savalas, who was very much absorbed in this interrogation.

McGinnis turned back to his witness, who seemed to be slumping in his chair like a bag of potatoes.

"Don't worry, Anselm. You're doing a great job. You are doing the right thing. We will make sure that the right person gets arrested, and they don't harm you."

"Assim would never harm me!" Anselm protested. "He's like the older brother that I never had. He loves me!"

"An older brother who is an anti-Semitist and homicide suspect?" McGinnis countered.

Anselm looked down.

"Let me just ask you one more question. At the time of the crime, which we believe happened between eleven PM and one AM on Sunday night, were you staying at Assim's house or your parents' house?"

Terrified of the consequences, but following his good intentions, Anselm answered correctly, "I was at Assim's house."

McGinnis pulled a fist in a gesture of victory. "Then are you able to tell us where the suspect was at the time mentioned?"

Hopelessly, Anselm looked at McGinnis. He shook his head and answered, "No. He wasn't home."

"Thank you very much, Anselm, you have helped us a lot! We will escort you back to your parents' home if you'd like."

"No, Detective. I don't need help. I can get home by myself," Anselm replied. He finished the water in the glass and stood up.

"Can I go now?"

"Yes, Anselm, you may leave now. But remember, if you notice anything suspicious, you call me."

McGinnis handed him his card, and warned him, "Be careful!"

Anselm checked out McGinnis' card, which read:

```
City of Pasadena
Crimes against people: Homicide Division
Detective Peter McGinnis
```

A cold shiver ran through Anselm's body. He pocketed the card and took off as fast as he could.

***

Left alone in the interrogation room, McGinnis sat down and took off his newsboy hat. He turned it upside down and looked at the inside as though there was something to be found in there.

"Heck!" He exclaimed out loud, "I think I'm getting old. How could I have overlooked that?!"

He jumped up from his seat and placed the hat back on his aging, but not yet senile cranium. Savalas came back in.

"What's going on Detective? You forgot something?"

"I most definitely did. Has anyone checked to see if there was any surveillance system installed? If there was a camera, maybe the evidence can be found there!"

"No, sorry, McGinnis. I'm afraid the forensics team already wrote in their report that there wasn't any kind of security system installed whatsoever."

Discouraged, McGinnis sat back down. "Damn! All we need is one little piece of evidence, and this case is over. I mean, what about footprints? Did anyone find anything relevant on the pathway from the old lady's house to Miss Robinson's yard?"

Savalas shook his head, "Not that I know of."

"Hmm." McGinnis didn't want to let it sit. "I'm going back to the crime scene. I want to see if I can find anything else."

"Sure thing, Detective. Meanwhile, I'll do the updates on the paperwork." Not that it was Savalas' favorite activity, but he'd frankly prefer to go for another dinner with Emma. But as long as the case wasn't solved, he couldn't contact her for private matters.

McGinnis got back up. "Thank you for that. You know my aversion to paperwork. Especially since it's all online these days. I really can't handle it that well anymore."

"Go outside and get some fresh air, McGinnis, I'll take care of it." McGinnis nodded with a tip of his newsboy hat and left.

***

Back in his Ford Futura, McGinnis once more headed toward Bungalow Heaven. He wondered, *what am I actually looking for?* He didn't know exactly why he wanted to go back to the crime scene. He just knew that he *had* to. Sometimes, in tough cases like these, McGinnis had learned to just follow his instincts. They usually proved accurate. That much he would grant himself credit for.

A speed bump on Wilson Street shook him out of his complacent daydreams. His hat tilted and almost fell off. He pushed it back into place. The sun was going down, and it blinded him. He passed in front of McDonald Park, and the playground was still filled with children of all ages. The ice-cream man had just left the playground, and a homeless guy shamelessly occupied a bench. Suddenly, McGinnis had an idea.

He inconspicuously parked the car alongside East Bell Street. It would be a little bit of a walk, but it would do him good.

He approached the homeless man on the bench. The man was a weatherbeaten middle-aged man, probably about McGinnis' age, but looked twenty years older. McGinnis felt pity for the unfortunate man.

"Please get up, Sir. I have a couple of questions for you," McGinnis said. He held his badge directly in front of the man's face, continuing without explaining too much. "I'm from the police."

While the homeless man overcame his first moment of shock—he probably thought that somebody was trying to chase him away again—he remembered that nobody could really ask him to leave his comfortable spot during the daytime. He made an effort to get up extra slowly.

"Can't nap in peace anymore," he complained. "I was just getting a little bit of sun on my face."

Not that he needed any more sun on his face, judging by its crinkled appearance. However, the wrinkles in this man's face were not caused by age. They were the result of who knows how many years of life on skid row.

"I'm from the homicide division, Sir. I have a couple of questions to ask you about Sunday night."

"Homicide? I ain't killed nobody," the homeless man instinctively defended himself.

"Not you. I am wondering if you saw or heard anything. Were you here?"

The homeless man preferred not to answer.

McGinnis helped him out. "The crime happened here," he said and turned around and pointed at house number 977.

"That the property where that dude with the big ass Infinity comes around?"

"Yes, Sir, that's exactly it. I'd just like to know. Did you hear or see anything suspicious on Sunday night?"

"I'm sorry, Detective. I really can't remember all that clearly."

McGinnis had a feeling he knew what direction this conversation was taking.

"Have some pity with an old man..." The homeless man extended his hand.

"We don't usually do that, the police, here. It's illegal, really," McGinnis explained as he instinctively started to scramble through his wallet.

"So, anything unusual?" McGinnis found a twenty and handed it to the homeless man.

"Sunday, you said?" The homeless man asked, and his attitude changed like a flipped coin.

McGinnis nodded, "Yes, Sir, on Sunday, between eleven PM and one AM."

"Come to think of it, I remember Sunday night quite well, because that's the night before my food bank opens. There was nothing unusual. The Infinity was showing off its big-ass nose as usual."

"The Infinity, you said? On Sunday?" McGinnis interrupted him.

The homeless guy nodded affirmatively. "The Infinity. It was parked there pretty much all night. But that's nothing unusual. That car is here often. At least, it's been that way for the past couple of weeks or so. That's why I noticed it. It's such a preposterous vehicle!"

"I see. Anything else? McGinnis asked.

"Somebody screamed. It must have been a nightmare, because the person stopped immediately, like people do when their minds wake up and they become aware that they've had a dream," the homeless man explained as he pocketed the money. He could most definitely use that. Then he hesitated.

"Wait a minute. You said homicide division?" Shocked, the homeless man was staring at him.

"Yes, Sir. Homicide."

"Maybe the person who I heard wasn't having a dream at all ," the homeless man realized.

"Maybe not," McGinnis said.

"Oh, my God!" Even for a tough man like the homeless guy, murder was a scary place to go in his mind.

"Thank you, Sir. You've helped us a great deal." In a routine movement, McGinnis handed him his card, saying, "Call me if you remember anything."

Stunned, the homeless man kept staring at the card issued by the notorious homicide division. He did not want anything to do with them, but he was too scared to throw it away. He pocketed the card.

McGinnis walked away. He did not even try to ask the man for his name, because he knew it was very unlikely that he would tell him the truth. He probably didn't have an ID on him. It would be easy to locate him in one of the homeless shelters, though, if ever they needed him as a witness. The detective hoped they wouldn't have to go so far.

Carefully, McGinnis approached the street and studied the crime scene again.

Now they had evidence that Assim was on the crime scene at the night of the murder. He would have a hard time explaining why he had been there. Then again, there was Maureen's hair in the entry hall. Not once had she denied having been there, although she did deny having committed the crime. Somehow, things were just still not matching up.

Was it possible that they were accomplices? Although that was possible, it was very unlikely. *Is there something I'm not seeing? There must be!*

McGinnis walked up and down by the two houses several times, combed through the front lawns, then through the backyards, and walked through the crime scene in the house once again. Even though he now had a good idea of what must have happened that night, he still couldn't figure out the motives.

Exhausted, he decided to try Emma Robinson again. Maybe she could lead him to the missing link.

***

It was almost dark. McGinnis knocked at the door of Emma's backhouse. He heard footsteps. *Lucky me*, he thought, *she's here!*

"Good evening, Detective!" Emma said. "Still no clues?" Emma asked, concerned when she saw how tired he looked. She had been absorbed in reading one of her clients' works, a Sherlock Holmes variation.

"We have more clues than we had at the beginning of the week, but if you don't mind, I would like to ask you a couple of questions before we interrogate our suspects again tomorrow."

"Of course, Detective, come on in." She put her pen and notebook down and walked into the kitchen. The flowers she had received from Savalas were beginning to wilt.

McGinnis felt like an intruder, marching in on her soft carpet with his heavy street shoes. "Should I take them off?" He asked feeling self-conscious.

Emma shook her head. "You can leave them on. I always do. It's only because I was settled in for the night that I'm in my slippers. And do forgive my wardrobe." She was wearing her pajamas and a cardigan.

McGinnis didn't mind. On the contrary, he couldn't stand women who thought they were in a permanent fashion show, perfectly dressed and made up all the time. Emma wasn't like that.

"Anything to drink, Detective? I was just making green tea," Emma said, and started to move around the cupboards, searching to replace the tea in the previously used kettle. She must have been drinking that stuff all night. Even though it was only green tea, McGinnis dreaded the caffeine. He was not much of a tea drinker as it was.

"A glass of water is fine," he said.

Slightly hurt in her pride as a good housekeeper, she held a glass under the water dispenser in her refrigerator. She grabbed a coaster and brought it to the round table.

"Have a seat!" she ordered, and the detective sat down. "How can I help you?"

"I know this must be painful for you, Miss Robinson, but I wondered if we couldn't go over the night of the crime. You went to see a movie with Miss Woodbridge, you said?"

"No more painful than spending a night in jail," Emma answered sarcastically.

McGinnis took a sip of water. This woman definitely had no fear of expressing herself. He gave her credit for that. Her outspokenness backed the impression of overall honesty that he had of her.

"We went to see *Jacky Robinson* after we found out *Life of Pi* wasn't running in the theaters anymore. It was my turn to pick the movie, so I was worried that she didn't like my choice. She was unusually quiet that night, and I didn't understand why. I still don't, to tell you the truth. Aunt Nettie was always very talkative."

"Well, that's something I haven't heard yet," McGinnis commented on the new piece of information. He took another sip of water. "And you have no idea why she was quiet?"

Emma shook her head. "I thought for a moment that she might be sick. But I asked her, and she said she was all right. I tried to deflect her lousy mood by talking about the property manager, but that didn't work either."

McGinnis listened carefully. Something about this information sounded familiar.

"What was her relation to the property manager? Were they on friendly terms, do you know?"

"Oh, yes!" Emma almost shouted. "She talked about him all the time. Only on Sunday night, she didn't mention him at all, and that was strange."

McGinnis's investigative brain was starting to operate.

"Oh, and that's why you thought that she was maybe developing feelings for him?"

"Yes, for a moment I thought about that. But frankly, I can barely understand how *anyone* could like a slimeball like Assim Esfahani. No reflection on his father, though. Ray's great!"

"Have you thought of the possibility that something Mr. Esfahani said to Miss Woodbrige that day might have upset her?"

Emma thought about the question for a long time; then she took a sip of green tea from her mug.

"Actually, it hasn't occurred to me at all, in that way. I mean, yes, of course it's possible. But what?"

Detective McGinnis finished his water and said, "Miss Robinson, unfortunately, I don't know. But hopefully, our second interrogation of the suspects will bring some more light on the question."

McGinnis got up and tiptoed to the door as softly as he could in his heavy urban street shoes. *They could definitely use a shine*, he noticed as he looked down at them. This woman was reminding him way too much of his domestic shortcomings, and he decided that he needed to leave quickly.

"Thank you, Miss Robinson. This conversation has been very helpful. If we figure out anything, I will let you know."

Emma got up and followed him to the door.

"Mr. McGinnis!" The detective had already stepped out the door.

"Yes, Miss?" He turned around.

"I would appreciate if somebody could inform me about the funeral of Mrs. Woodbridge. I would like to attend, but I have not been given any information about it whatsoever."

"Oh, of course!" He smiled. "I will have someone call you tomorrow."

"And say hello to Lieutenant Savalas!" She shouted. She knew now that the lunch had been set up by McGinnis for no purpose at all, except for them to get to know each other. Anything else just didn't make sense.

"Will do!" The detective promised, and tipped on his hat to say goodbye. Emma closed the door.

She was relieved that was over for the evening. She was an altogether peaceful person, and wished these interrogations would end very soon. She poured herself another cup of freshly brewed green tea, sat down, and continued reading the manuscript.

***

Heading back to his car, McGinnis tried to make sense of the scene that Emma just had described. Tired of trying to find the missing piece of the puzzle, McGinnis finally gave up. He decided that only another interrogation of both suspects would bring any progress to the case, especially with the new evidence that he had. Assim wasn't going to like it, but he'd better not run away again or he could not be released on bail this time.

Relieved that the day was over, McGinnis got into his Ford Futura and drove home for the night. He looked forward to getting a good night's sleep. No time for Lucky Baldwin's tonight. Tim Simmons would have to wait.

# Revealing More

The next morning, Detective McGinnis returned to headquarters in a rather grumpy mood. It was Friday, and this case was still not solved. He did not want to spend another weekend without Nell.

Out of breath, he entered the office area on the second floor. He had again used the steps. His experience at the fitness studio, trying in vain to catch up to Assim and Savalas, had rung a sad bell. *Maybe I should sign up there for a tryout.* He took off his simple green jacket, and instinctively refuted the thought.

Savalas came his way. He was quite an early bird, McGinnis noticed and felt lucky again to have such a great lieutenant at hand.

"Morning, Detective. Anything new on the case?"

"Morning, Savalas. Not sure yet. Maybe. We have to do a second interrogation of the suspects today."

"That's what I thought was the plan. You want me to bring the first one in?"

Savalas walked the detective to his office.

"Apparently, the old lady was quite fond of the property manager. But then again, you already told me that on Wednesday, didn't you?" said McGinnis.

"Yes, that's what Emma told me."

"Yes, but you didn't mention that the old lady was acting differently on their movie night. You always have to report all the details, not just your conclusions. Got it, Lieutenant?"

Savalas nodded and said, "Got it, McGinnis."

"I'm supposed to bring you regards from Emma, by the way," the detective snickered as he hung his green jacket on the coat rack and adjusted his hat. They were entering his cramped cubicle. Savalas did not know what to say.

He decided to change the topic. "You want me to bring the suspects in now?"

The detective nodded.

"Which one first?"

McGinnis considered for a minute. "Bring in the property manager. His car's been seen on the night of the crime."

"Really?" Savalas had no idea. "Where would I find him?" Savalas dreaded another car chase.

"Try calling his lawyer. He'll make sure he shows up promptly. After the scene he made the other day, I don't think Assim's going to cause much trouble anymore. At least I hope not."

McGinnis handed Dr. Elias Fahrad's business card to him. It had his phone number embossed at the bottom.

"This should make things easier."

"Consider it done," Savalas said. He grabbed the card and went into his own cubicle.

"Alrighty then," said the detective and started rubbing his hands together in quiet anticipation.

***

Thirty minutes later, Savalas went into the interrogation room with a visibly perturbed property manager and Dr. Elias Fahrad in tow. Assim wasn't looking so good today. His ego was bruised, and the troubles showed in his barely perfect face. Regardless of the lawyer's presence, Savalas still had to struggle to get Assim to follow.

When the suspect finally sat down, Savalas looked at McGinnis. He was quietly observing the situation from the corner of the room, ready for further instruction. He nodded slightly, which meant that Savalas should let him go on with the interrogation. Savalas positioned himself at the door because he didn't trust this guy for a second.

When everyone was settled in, McGinnis took off his hat, scratched his head, put the hat back on, and approached the suspect, who looked very angry.

"According to our latest investigations, your car was seen at the crime scene at the time of the crime. It would interest me to hear what explanation you have for that, Mr. Esfahani!"

The revelation of that bitter fact seemed to awaken Assim out of his angry daze.

"Oh, yes? Who said that?"

"Sorry, Mr. Esfahani, I'm afraid I cannot reveal that piece of information to you. Besides, I'm the one who's asking the questions here. So?"

Assim looked back at the detective spitefully. Dr. Fahrad took over the conversation. "As long as you don't have any specific proof, Detective McGinnis, I have advised my client to remain silent."

"I see," McGinnis said angrily, but he just ignored the lawyer's presence and spoke directly to Assim.

"You're stubborn. But let me tell you something. Whether you talk or not, we are going to find the truth. Opening your mouth is just going to alleviate your situation. It's going to take you years to get your driver's license back after what you did the other day. If you ask me, it doesn't look very good in the world of real estate when you don't have a car to drive to the properties you are trying to sell."

"I don't need anyone to tell me how to do my job," Assim screamed.

*Maybe he does,* McGinnis thought. He was amazed at how some people managed to dig their own grave mound when they were already stuck on the bottom of the hole.

Savalas and McGinnis exchanged a glance. "Bring in the other suspect!" He ordered.

Before he left the room, Savalas walked up to McGinnis and whispered something into his ear. McGinnis agreed with a frown.

Savalas left the room. Another officer entered and stood in front of the door. McGinnis didn't need a babysitter, but since Savalas insisted, he wouldn't make a scene. He just wanted to move forward today.

***

Minutes later, Savalas was back with Maureen Dorsay, who looked like she hadn't shut an eye all night. Her hair was all tangled and she had dark circles under her eyes, revealing her sadness. Her makeup was smudged, and she had visibly spent the night crying. Savalas almost felt sorry for her. He placed her on the other side of the table, just like the last time. He was still mad that she had made him chase her down the road. She could have just turned herself in; he had to be careful not to be too rough with her out of anger.

Once she sat down and appeared relatively steady, he took off her cuffs.

"Well, thank you very much, Lieutenant," she said sarcastically.

Savalas didn't respond. He just quietly placed himself next to the other officer in front of the door. He didn't ask him to leave, just in case—the situation might escalate.

"Good morning, Mrs. Dorsay," the detective greeted her, lifting his hat. He used the opportunity to gently stroke his semi-bald head, a habit he'd acquired many years ago, along with wearing a hat.

"You look like you didn't have a very restorative night," he commented.

"Ha-ha," she laughed back into his face.

*These suspects have no respect*, he thought and concluded that he needed to change his method of inquiry if he ever wanted to get anywhere with this case.

"Mrs. Dorsay, up until this moment, I have been very gentle and considerate with you, and I continue to face nothing but a lack ofcooperation and spiteful behavior. I can also act differently."

Maureen looked at him, obviously fearful. McGinnis knew that she was afraid; there was no doubt about it. He just didn't know why.

"So let me ask you again, Mrs. Dorsay. With the crisis in the relationship with your husband, are you currently seeing someone else on the side?"

Maureen looked down in shame. "Mrs. Dorsay, Mr. Esfahani's car was seen parked alongside Mrs. Woodbridge's house on the night the murder happened. Have you and Mr. Esfahani been seeing each other behind your husband's back?" McGinnis wanted to know.

"This question goes for you, too Mr. Esfahani. It would at least helpexplain why your car was seen close to the victim's home at the time of the murder."

Dr. Fahrad quickly whispered something to Assim, who laughed out loud and fell back into silence. He gave Maureen a threatening look.

"Mrs. Dorsay, one does not get arrested for having a simple marital affair, even if the person you are sleeping with is a murderer. But one does get arrested for obstruction of the law, and if you continue to withhold information from us, I will be forced to keep you in here until you begin to cooperate. I hate to do this to you, but you need to start telling us the truth, or you might spend the rest of your lifetime behind bars because of the actions of another person. Do you want that?"

Maureen was cornered. There was no way out of this, especially since not even her lawyer knew what had happened.

"No, I don't!" Maureen finally said. "I didn't do it. Assim killed her, and I can prove it!"

Shocked, Assim looked at her for the first time, and then he looked down again.

"No you can't!" he snickered meanly. Dr. Fahrad had tried to silence him, but Assim was faster.

"Yes, I can! It's all on my phone! I filmed the whole scene, starting from when you broke in, to when you took the menorah, to the actual crime. I have the whole thing on my iPhone."

Assim got up and threatened her. Dr. Fahrad tried to hold him back, but he only got pushed back into his chair. "No, you cannot!" Assim screamed.

Savalas had to pin him down, because he was about to attack Maureen. She was fearful and withdrew in the chair. Savalas had a hard time wrestling Assim back into his chair, but he finally managed with the aid of the other officer.

"Now you're talking, Maureen. That's the type of answers I've been looking for."

"She's lying!" Assim protested. Dr. Fahrad was pouring sweat. There was no reasoning with his client in this state of anger.

"Mr. Esfahani, I told you to be quiet!" he tried instructing him.

"No, I'm not. I'm *not* lying, and you know it!" Maureen screamed back.

"Don't listen to her, Mr. Ginnis, the woman is lying!" Assim yelled and tried to get up, but he couldn't because his restraints and his hands cuffed behind his back made it impossible.

"Get him out of here, Savalas! We don't have time for this right now."

"I got him," Savalas said and ordered the other cop to assist him. Together, they dragged the protesting property manager out of the room and moved him into a holding cell. Assim wasn't looking so good at this point. Dr. Fahrad followed. He was visibly perturbed.

Before the cops managed to get Assim out of the interrogation room, he turned around and looked Maureen straight in the eye. "I will kill you, Maureen. Trust me, I will!"

Savalas and the other officer dragged him out. They shut the door.

McGinnis aired his head out again by lifting the hat up and down. "Now, that was interesting," he commented, completely emotionless. "You have evidence, you said?"

Terrified and pale, Maureen nodded. "Yes, I filmed the whole scene. I didn't believe he would do it, that's why I didn't call the cops right away. I wish I had. But yes, I should have it all on my phone."

"Where's your phone right now, Maureen?"

"Confiscated."

"Excellent!" McGinnis shouted. "So we have it." He buzzed Savalas, who had just finished stuffing the Persian bully back into a holding cell.

"Lieutenant, can you get Maureen's phone, please?"

"Where is it?"

"It's with us, together with all her other things."

"It's probably run out of power by now," Maureen warned.

McGinnis considered the comment. "Oh, and bring a charger along, too."

"Consider it done," Savalas said, and hung up. He was glad things were moving forward today.

Five minutes later, Savalas was back in the interrogation room with Maureen's iPhone and a charger.

"This yours?" Savalas asked just for formality's sake.

She took one look at the rhinestone phone case and recognized it instantly. "Yes, that's mine," she confirmed.

"Bring it over here!" McGinnis ordered. It was sitting on the side of the interrogation table that was equipped with a whole arsenal of electrical plugs.

McGinnis grabbed the phone from Savalas' hand like a starving vulture and quickly plugged it in. Savalas stood by him as the detective switched it on and searched for the video.

"You know how to get the video?" she asked. Maureen had started to show her more cooperative side, and McGinnis liked it. Nevertheless, he gave her a look that could kill, because he also didn't like to be treated like a baby. He was not easy to deal with. *Don't mess with me; I can do this*, he thought. *I am not as old as I look.* He continued to poke around the phone like a child with a newfound toy.

"Here!" Savalas stopped him.

"It's the last video I made," Maureen commented.

"Obviously."

"I think we got it, Mrs. Dorsay."

Like two kids in a game store, McGinnis and Savalas squeezed together, staring at the screen of their newfound evidence. McGinnis pressed play.

# Indisputable Evidence

Almost in disbelief, Lieutenant Savalas and Detective McGinnis stared at the screen of the iPhone. There it was, playing right in front of them, the piece of evidence that they'd been looking for all week.

The video started from where Assim entered through the backyard, continuing as he walked across the yard and quietly snuck in through the back door.

Then, Natalie Woodbridge kisses Emma goodbye and is about to close the door, when Assim enters the living room and picks up the menorah. Natalie hears something in the background and is so startled to see the property manager that she forgets to close the door. She said, "Mr. Esfahani, why are you here?"

Assim has gloves on. He tightens his grip on the menorah and walks toward her menacingly. "You shouldn't peek in on other people's properties," Assim says, and takes one step closer.

"I didn't mean to spy on you. I was just bringing her cake. If I had known, I would never have..."

But it's too late. Natalie Woodbridge will never amend whatever might have gone wrong on that day.

Coldheartedly, Assim whacks her over the head before she can finish her sentence. Natalie lets out a short scream of pain and falls to the ground, unconscious. Her head is bleeding slightly.

"Stupid woman!" Assim says, and hits her over the head again, and again, and again and again, until the blood comes streaming down over her entire face and body. Assim quickly gets up and does a self-check for blood on his clothing. Safe. He takes a look at the murder weapon.

"Take it to the blonde next door. That should cause some confusion," he said out loud.

He exits the house through the back door—the same way he came in—and simply throws the weapon over the fence. He takes off his gloves and walks to the car. End of video.

***

Detective McGinnis silently put down the phone. He exchanged a meaningful glance with Lieutenant Savalas. Then he looked at Maureen, sadly.

"Why not right away?" McGinnis scolded her. "You know how much trouble you put me through, and the lieutenant?"

He made a gesture at Savalas, who nodded in consent.

"I was scared," Maureen explained.

"Scared of Mr. Esfahani?"

Maureen nodded.

"But we had him safely locked up in his holding cell! At least on the day that we interrogated you! Why, Maureen? Why hold back on such important information?"

"I was scared because of the consequences! That is why I didn't call the cops," Maureen started talking.

"Why didn't you call us, then? I'd like to know. And I would appreciate if you could be as specific as possible."

"You don't know the whole story, Mr. Ginnis."

"Well, then tell us what happened, Maureen. We're not going anywhere. We have all day, and all night, too, if necessary. Just don't try playing any games with us anymore. It's going to be difficult enough not to consider you an accomplice under the circumstances. And my name is McGinnis, just for your records!"

McGinnis took off his hat and shook his head. *Why is it so difficult for people to remember my name?* He didn't get it.

Maureen let out a sigh of relief. *No matter how much trouble I'm in, it's still better than letting that evil man run free.*

McGinnis put his hat back on and looked at her. "You can go ahead now. Tell us everything. And don't play any tricks. We'll notice it."

"All right, all right, Detective. Calm down. I'll tell you what happened."

For the first time in this interrogation process, McGinnis was able to sit down. "All right, Maureen. Tell us your story."

Savalas continued to control the door. *You never know with these loonies, besides, it's my job to keep the place safe.*

"It all began when Alan came home drunk again, three weeks ago. The smell of his breath and his hurtful words were too much."

"What did he say?" McGinnis scratched his head and put his hat back on.

"He called me an infertile old maid."

As Maureen was speaking, McGinnis' lower jaw started to chew on his upper lip. Then he stopped.

"What did you tell him?"

"I got mad and told him that I had been taking the pill all along. I invited him to look into my half of the medicine cabinet and check it out."

"And then?"

"When he came back from the bathroom after he'd found the truth, he started attacking me. He was trying to hit me, but I'd already grabbed my coat and shoes before he came back, and since he was drunk, all I had to do was push him back, and he fell. Alan was not the strongest of men."

"Did he follow you outside?"

"No. When he was down on the floor, I told him that he was a fool, and there was no way I was going to have a baby with him, drinking the way he was. I told him that he needed to get sober, or I'd leave him."

"What did he say?"

"Nothing. He just stared at me. Then I walked out the door and ran into Assim, who was collecting his rent. I pretty much crashed into him."

"What happened then?"

"By the time I was outside, I was bawling, overflowing with tears. He told me that he was finished collecting his money, and he invited me out for a drink."

Savalas and McGinnis exchanged a glance.

"I had no bad intentions at all! I was just grateful to have somebody to talk to. One thing led to another. I got pretty drunk and the next thing I knew, I woke up naked in a bed of red silk. After all the crap and the bad sex I'd been through with Alan, it felt good to let go like that."

"You went back there?"

With shame, Maureen nodded.

"I was at his place almost every other night."

"Did Alan know you were having an affair?"

Maureen shook her head and said, "I don't think so. Or maybe he did, I don't know."

"Why do you think he was continuing the adoption process even though you told him that you weren't interested in adopting children with him?"

Maureen looked up and sighed. "*You* try reasoning with an alcoholic! I don't know. I think he was just painfully holding onto something that he'd lost long ago."

"You!" McGinnis took off his hat again, gently wiped across his semi-bald head and put his hat back on again.

Maureen shrugged.

"Let's get back to the case. What happened on the night of the murder? Why did Assim tell Natalie she shouldn't peek in on other people's properties? Do you know anything about that? Can you explain that sentence?"

"Natalie looked through my window while we were doing it in the living room."

Savalas and McGinnis exchanged another rather startled glance.

"Natalie was holding a cake in her hand. When she saw us, she must have dropped it. I went to the door right away, but she had already left. She must have felt so terribly ashamed of me. There was chocolate all over the bushes. I cleaned it away later."

McGinnis looked at Savalas. The lieutenant knew what that meant. They needed to send a forensics team to Maureen's front door and have them check for evidence of chocolate cake.

"If you'll excuse us for a moment. I have something I need to discuss with the lieutenant."

McGinnis got up and led Savalas out the door. He carefully locked the door from the hallway. They stood in front of the interrogation room.

"You gonna call Dr. Pepperstone, or do I?"

"I'll do it, "Savalas said. "You're in the midst of conducting an interrogation. I'll have a forensics team sent over ASAP to take some samples. I'll also have someone else sent over here, for a reconciliation."

Savalas made a gesture to the woman sitting inside.

"Good thinking, Savalas."

"Consider it done," Savalas said and walked down the hallway to his office, where he was going to make some phone calls. McGinnis went back into the interrogation room. Normally, he wouldn't just walk in there unprotected. He felt he had nothing to fear from Maureen, though.

***

McGinnis quietly re-entered the interrogation room and asked, "What happened next?"

McGinnis took off his hat and sat down. Maureen was still in the same position, humbled to tears.

McGinnis offered her a tissue from the box on the table. "Here!"

Maureen cleaned her nose and went on to say, "I wanted to follow her and apologize for what she saw, but I was not dressed, and when I went back to gather my clothes, Assim was cussing her out like nothing I'd ever heard before."

"Like what?"

A quiet knock on the door indicated that Savalas had finished his task. McGinnis got up and let him in.

Savalas took the same spot in front of the door as before. McGinnis, hatless, sat back down.

"Like what, Mrs. Dorsay?"

"He called her a stupid Jew,'" Maureen said and then she glanced around the room as if she was afraid that somebody had heard her. She looked down in shame.

"What else did he say?"

"He started saying how he was tired of Jews perpetually ruining his life, since childhood. I had no clue what he meant. He also said that today was the last day that Natalie had benefited by living on Ray's property."

Exhausted, Maureen leaned her elbows on the table and grabbed her hair. Tears started streaming down her face again. McGinnis and Savalas exchanged a glance.

"I wish I had called the police right away, especially now. But I was so full of shame, and I didn't know what to tell them. I was afraid they would think I was crazy!"

"Did you know he was going to kill her that night?"

"No, I mean, yes, maybe. I didn't know for sure, but I was worried. When I heard his car pulling up again on Sunday night, I got curious. I didn't know how to help the old lady. So I sneaked over and filmed him. That's why you found the hair. I was going to film what he did to her, but once I saw her and realized she was dead, I got so horrified I couldn't do it. I panicked and ran away."

"Why didn't you call the police then?"

Maureen was weeping heavily. She looked at the detective; her eyes were filled with nothing but sorrow. "I wish I had, but I couldn't. I was too afraid. I wanted to call them the whole time that Assim was in there, but I was filming. Once I pressed the start button, I couldn't stop. It was like I was tied to my iPhone."

"Some religious people might say that it was your higher power that kept your finger on that button, Mrs. Dorsay. Regardless, whether you called the police or not, your arguments may not be valid, but they are understandable, and that piece of evidence that you just gave is your ticket out of jail. I doubt very much that any judge will hold anything severe against you, under the circumstances."

Maureen let out a big sigh of relief, tears streaming down her face once more. McGinnis handed her another tissue.

"We do need you to tell us what you did next, just for matters of completeness. What did you do after you discovered that Natalie Woodbridge could no longer be helped?"

Maureen finished blowing her nose and struggled to answer. "I ran back into my house, packed a bunch of clothes, and drove to my aunt's house. That's where I stayed, until you found me."

"Was your husband concerned about you when he didn't find you in your home upon his arrival?"

Sadly, Maureen shook her head no and said, "I don't know. I think he was mad. But after the scene I had with him earlier this month, my absence was no surprise. I told him that I needed a few days away from him, to reconsider our marriage."

A questioning glance was thrown at Maureen, who answered it with another sigh. "I don't think he was too happy about it, but what can you do? I told him that he needed to get sober if he wanted to stay married to me."

"Have you seen your husband since?"

Maureen shook her head again and said, "I don't even think he knows I'm here."

McGinnis glanced at Savalas, who nodded and exited the room. Two minutes later, he escorted Alan Foster into the room.

"Mrs. Dorsay, we figured you might want to talk to your husband for a little bit. He claims he has been sober since the day you walked out on him."

Maureen's jaw dropped open at the unexpected sight of her husband, who was frozen in shock to see his wife at all, and especially seeing her broken down like this. A few moments of silence seemed loud between them, and no words could be exchanged. Finally, Alan began to speak.

"I'm so sorry, Maureen. All this happened because of me!" Alan opened his arms, ready to embrace his wife. He explained, "I've been sober for twenty-six days now, honey. What you told me about the pill, the anti-baby pill, made me realize that I needed to quit drinking. It was a sobering experience. I haven't touched a drop of alcohol since."

Overwhelmed by her husband's sincerity, Maureen got up and fell into his arms.

# Off and Away

Friday morning, case closed—almost. McGinnis sat in his office scratching his head. The newsboy hat was laying on the desk. Savalas was taking his morning break. He hadn't taken a break all week. The case was solved, but their job was far from being finished.

While McGinnis was sitting there chewing on his upper lip, Savalas walked in with a cup of machine brewed coffee in each hand.

"Coffee, Detective?"

McGinnis was surprised by the friendly offer. This young man was paying attention.

"Oh thanks, Savalas. What do I owe you?"

Lieutenant Savalas vehemently shook his head. "We still have a lot of work to do before the weekend, and I figured you could use a pick-me-up."

"That's good thinking, Lieutenant,"McGinnis said and took a sip. It was a loud, shameless slurp. Savalas snickered. He knew it couldn't be easy for a woman to live with this man.

"Have a seat!" McGinnis ordered. Savalas pulled out the old hydraulic wood chair and lowered it. For some reason, each time he sat down there, he felt like he was back at school again. McGinnis studied him quietly.

***

Cramped in McGinnis' windowless office, they more or less silently finished their coffees. When they were done, McGinnis held up the trash can.

"In here!" McGinnis ordered. Savalas did a slam-dunk.

"Ready for trouble?" McGinnis stopped chewing on his upper lip and put his hat back on.

"Fahrad got Assim out on bail again. We have to collect him for the final confrontation with the evidence."

Savalas nodded. "Let's go!"

On their way to the squad car, they grabbed two other officers for support. They followed in another squad car.

With their team all lined up, they headed once more into the brick building on Corson Street.

Before they even went in, they sent the second patrol car to the entrance on Summit Avenue. Savalas was not going to make the mistake of leaving any escape route uncovered again.

McGinnis entered the building with Savalas by his side. Without a word, both cops showed their badges to the receptionist on duty, the same Asian giant as last time. He let them pass without a question.

The lieutenant was the only one in uniform, so the badges were appropriate. The receptionist would have had the right to stop them if they hadn't flashed them.

"We need to go to Adon & Co. one more time. Which floor is that, again?" McGinnis tried to ask the giant.

"Third," Savalas answered before the receptionist could. Then they stepped inside the elevator, which had been programmed to go to the third floor by pressing the buttons on the outside—another technological innovation McGinnis couldn't figure out.

Savalas and McGinnis energetically got off the elevator and headed to the reception area at Adon & Co. with their badges drawn, and hands on their weapons.

The petite Latina stared at them in disbelief. They didn't give her a second glance. They were there for Assim.

"City of Pasadena Police. Don't move, or I will arrest you for real," McGinnis threatened.

The young lady barely dared breathe, until the two cops were around the corner. Once they were out of sight, the daredevil picked up the intercom and called Assim.

McGinnis and Savalas had found his office before she made that call. Their entry caused quite a stir in the large law office. The two lawyers who happened to be at their desks curiously peeked around the corners to see what was happening.

Savalas knocked on the door and announced: "Police! Open the door, or we will enter forcefully."

They gave it a second. They could hear whispers and a stir of activity.

"Open!" McGinnis ordered.

Savalas tried the doorknob quietly, with his gun drawn. Yes, it was unlocked. McGinnis gave him cover from behind.

They entered in a rush. When they entered, both men, Anselm on the left and Assim in front of them, had risen from their chairs. A black suitcase was sitting on Assim's desk.

"Everybody freeze! Mr. Esfahani, you are under arrest for the murder of Natalie Woodbridge! You have the right..." McGinnis shouted, but he was briskly interrupted.

Assim and Anselm stood there with their hands up. They seemed prepared. Assim glanced at the suitcase. "Take that to Elias Farhad," Assim ordered.

Anselm nodded without saying a word, and obediently kept his arms over his head.

Savalas walked over to Assim's side and had pulled out the handcuffs with one hand, when suddenly Assim grabbed Savalas' gun arm. He twisted the arm behind Savalas' back, took the gun from him, and aimed it at McGinnis. "If I were you, Mr. Ginnis, I wouldn't shoot—provided the life of your colleague means anything to you."

McGinnis had no choice. He dropped his weapon. Although he knew that Savalas was wearing his bulletproof vest, he didn't want to risk the lieutenant's safety unnecessarily.

"The name is McGinnis, God damn it! And don't worry, Mr. Esfahani. You might have won the first round, but we will get you sooner or later. Probably sooner, rather than later. It wouldn't be the first time we had to hunt down someone unstable like you."

But McGinnis' words went unheard. Instead, he heard a loud *thwack*. Assim had smacked Savalas across the jaw with the gun, knocking him down to the floor.

Assim took off running. McGinnis was annoyed. *Why can nobody ever remember my name?*

Savalas was coming around, and he was seeing stars. McGinnis helped him up and asked, "You all right, Buddy?"

Savalas' nose was bleeding. His left eye was already developing a gigantic shiner. McGinnis handed him his handkerchief.

"I'll be fine. I'm just worried about him walking around with that gun of mine."

"Here!" McGinnis bent down and pulled out his spare Beretta P4 from his ankle holster. By the time he was upright again, McGinnis was panting. He could definitely use some exercise.

"What the...?" Savalas gawked. "According to my knowledge, cops in Pasadena are only allowed one gun per person."

"That's private property. You better not lose that one, too. It has emotional value," McGinnis explained.

"I won't. Promise!"

"Come on, Savalas, let's go!" Savalas pulled himself together.

"And you, my friend," McGinnis turned around to address Anselm: "I'll talk to you later!"

The two cops dashed out of the offices, running toward the main entrance. The only other entrance was covered by the other two officers.

"Any clue where he's heading?" Savalas asked as they ran down the fire escape.

"Yes, *a* clue. One. But let's try to catch him, first!"

***

Savalas came bursting out of the door of the fire escape, closely followed by McGinnis. The giant receptionist watched them with awe, and without a word exchanged, he just pointed toward the main entrance. "That way!"

"You got some extra time at hand?" McGinnis shouted at the feisty Asian, desperately trying to catch his breath. The giant nodded.

"Tell my colleagues at the other door to meet us at the crime scene on Wilson Street."

"Will do, Sir!" The receptionist saluted. Savalas and McGinnis took off. Just as they exited through the glass door, they saw the maroon Infinity speeding up Corson Street.

"Come on, Savalas, let's catch him! That fool ain't goin' nowhere," McGinnis said. They ran to their squad car.

"You know where he's headed?" Savalas asked, astonished.

"Pretty sure. Let's head to Wilson Street, the assistant's house. I have the feeling more trouble awaits us there."

"If you say so!" Savalas said, and started the motor. Sometimes, McGinnis was a walking mystery to him.

# Kidnapped

"I knew it!" McGinnis sighed as he loaded his SIG Sauer.

Assim's SUV was parked in front of Emma's Craftsman, and somebody had just shut her door.

"You knew that he was going after her?"

McGinnis nodded and hopped out of the passenger seat. He kept the door open to use it as a shield.

"Call the SWAT team, and hand me that loudspeaker."

"You're not gonna wait for the SWAT guys to arrive?" Savalas asked.

McGinnis shook his head. Savalas was baffled. The detective could be such a desk rat, and then suddenly, out of nowhere, his superhero instincts came back to life. Savalas secretly wished he *was* more like McGinnis, right now anyway. He was more of a pragmatist, though. He would wait for the SWAT team. However, an order was order, and he made the call. When he was done, he handed the loudspeaker to McGinnis.

"Mr. Esfahani! We know you're in there. Come out with your hands raised, or we will enter forcefully."

McGinnis awaited a response. No response came.

He repeated, "Mr. Esfahani. We know you have the girl. Come out with your hands raised, and leave the girl alone. You are only making it worse for yourself!"

Again, no response. Instead, they heard a crash and a squeaking sound, like from opening an old door.

"McGinnis! They're going out through the back! That was the sound of the back door!"

"Let's get him!" McGinnis ordered. "He won't make it beyond the property, even with the girl."

McGinnis and Savalas quickly moved toward the door of Emma's Craftsman. Meanwhile, the SWAT team had arrived. McGinnis gave them orders to hold a position in the front while Savalas and McGinnis entered the house, doing a quick check to the left and right. Just as Savalas had assumed, the kitchen's back door was standing ajar.

When the two cops arrived in the back yard, Assim was halfway up the wall. Emma was standing beside him on the ground.

"Mr. Esfahani! Don't move, or I'll shoot!"

Assim continued to climb the stone wall.

McGinnis fired his gun. Emma screamed, and Assim, shocked by the loud crack and her shriek, slipped and dropped from the wall. McGinnis had missed on purpose. He had just been trying to get Assim off the wall. He had completed his mission successfully.

Quickly, Savalas rushed toward Emma and pulled her away. McGinnis crossed the yard, keeping his weapon aimed at Assim. Savalas carefully disarmed him.

"Don't move!" he warned him.

Assim was defeated.

"Up, now!" McGinnis ordered. He was furious. Assim's escapades were costing not only too much of his time, they were also costing the Pasadena police department a considerable amount of unnecessary money.

Savalas grabbed his handcuffs for the second time while McGinnis continued to point his gun at Assim's emotionless but attractive face.

"Step away Emma, it's not safe!" Savalas ordered.

Emma took two steps back. She didn't need to be any closer to that monster of a man than necessary. Besides, when he perspired, he smelled.

Savalas took his turn in twisting Assim's arms to cuff him behind his back, and he was not gentle. This bully definitely could not be trusted.

"You have the right to remain silent..." Savalas started to read his rights.

"Stupid cops!" Assim yelled. "Elias will get me out here before the night is over. You are *so* wasting your time!"

"I sincerely doubt that, Mr. Esfahani," McGinnis proudly announced, escorting the culprit to the car. "I'm afraid the evidence against you is indisputable," McGinnis explained.

"What evidence?" Assim asked, followed by a litany of curse words. Some were spoken in English, and some in Farsi. McGinnis and Savalas had to drag him, more or less.

Once they arrived back at their police cruiser, McGinnis called the SWAT team to back off. They had managed on their own, as usual.

# Indisputable Guilt

Back at headquarters, Savalas dragged Assim into the holding cell with the help of another officer. They would be holding him there until McGinnis was ready for the final interrogation.

McGinnis was on his way to the interrogation room. He slowly sauntered down the hallway, then came to an abrupt stop and turned around.

He retraced his steps and knocked on the door of the last office in the row, where the stately letters Chief of Police Barthold Meane were embossed in gold on an old wooden door. While the stains on the letters of the upper line proved the many centuries this word had been posted there, the lower line had scratch marks on its letters and its gold was polished and shiny, revealing its more ephemeral character. The chief of police in the city of Pasadena was interchangeable.

McGinnis, who couldn't avoid noting this newness of the lower letters with a sense of deeper wisdom, knocked carefully.

"Come in!" A calm, but high-pitched voice said.

In front of him sat his superior Mr. Barthold Meane, poring over a new book. *Unbelievable, how tax money is wasted in state administration,* McGinnis thought. *This guy has literally nothing to do!*

"Ah, my favorite detective of all time. How can I help you, McGinnis?"

*At least he's able to say my name right,* McGinnis reluctantly thought.

"We're closing up the case, Chief. Wanna listen to the interrogation of the culprit? He hasn't admitted to the crime yet, which could still relieve him of a considerable amount of years, if he did. Routine procedure."

"You got proof?" Barthold Meane swung his legs off the table and closed the book.

McGinnis gave him a smug nod.

"Yes, Chief, one of the suspects had it on video all along. She was just too scared to come out with the evidence."

"Who did it? Wait! Let me guess! The assistant who pretended to be all nice and saintly?" Barthold asked as if he were the audience of a mystery story.

McGinnis shook his head. *This guy is so out of line.*

"Guess again."

Barthold Meane mentally pressed the rewind button on the interrogation that he had seen but couldn't figure out.

"Or just come with me. You'll see."

Without hesitation, Barthold Meane followed McGinnis.

"Oh, and you can call in the media conference as planned? Don't expect me to say anything, though; you know how I am."

"Don't worry, McGinnis, I'll do that part. That's my job. Oh, and excellent work, McGinnis!" McGinnis received a very hesitant pat on his shoulders.

Except for praising or scolding and making a good impression in front of the media, Bartholdo didn't do much good. Only a little bit less than annoyed than usual, because he had received praise for once, McGinnis led his boss into the observation room.

***

McGinnis was pacing up and down. The iPhone was kept safely on his side of the table. Of course, the file had been fact checked and verified for its authenticity by Dr. Pepperstone, who had also already made a copy of the file. He carefully slid the chip with the copy of the file into his suit jacket.

McGinnis slowed down when he heard loud voices and a clatter. *That must be them,* he thought.

A few seconds later, Savalas and the other officer came in, trying to keep the suspect from pushing them over. Assim was most definitely as strong as an ox.

When they finally managed to sit him down, Savalas handcuffed him to a rail that had been specially installed for just that purpose.

"Here he is. He's all yours, Detective!" Savalas said, with a sarcastic snicker. Both officers walked to the door, where they made sure that the suspect, or future convict, could never walk out.

Detective McGinnis cleared his throat a little and addressed Assim.

"Mr. Esfahani, in the course of our investigation, material has been found and verified which undeniably proves your immediate responsibility in the death of Mrs. Natalie Woodbridge."

Assim stared at McGinnis as if he had seen a ghost. He didn't say a word, just stared. If it hadn't been for the officers patrolling the door, McGinnis would have started to feel slightly uncomfortable. He simply moved forward.

"Now, do you chose to confess, or do you need to be confronted with the material standing against you, Mr. Esfahani?"

Again, an empty stare. "This is bullshit. You have nothing on me, Mr. Ginnis. I'm not saying a word without my lawyer."

"I'm sorry I have to reveal this evidence to you, Mr. Esfahani–and I do not choose to do this, but I am bound by law to give you one last chance to confess, which could considerably ameliorate the charges you are looking at in the future. So, do you choose to confess, Mr. Esfahani?"

Assim stubbornly shook his head no.

"All right then, Mr. Esfahani. Then let's take a look at this video."

The interrogation room was a modern, well-equipped facility that allowed them to project the video from the iPhone to the wall. For once in his life, McGinnis was grateful for modern technology. As he started the video, he decided he was actually starting to like this room.

"There you go..."

But Assim was already outraged. "Who did this video?" He screamed as the first scene started.

The video continued; the murderer entered the back door, and then his silhouette became visible in the living room. The next scene was of Emma saying goodbye to Aunt Nettie, and Natalie turned around.

"Did that bitch give you this?" Assim screamed. "This is a scam! I want to speak to Elias! I want Dr. Fahrad!"

The no longer so good-looking man's requests were silently denied, giving preference to the presentation of the film on the wall.

As the final scene of the murder played, the room fell silent. Assim was gaping at the screen, watching his gloved hands grip the menorah tighter and cold-heartedly slam it into the old woman's head again and again.

As the figure on the screen smashed the old lady's skull, while she was already laying on the floor, it seemed to McGinnis that a faint smile quirked up the corners of the suspect's mouth. McGinnis thought Assim's eyes began to shine as only those of an insane person could: no one sane could brighten upon witnessing brutality such as this.

"Go get her!" Assim whispered.

When he noticed that he had involuntarily commented on the evidence, he tried to get up and pull the handcuffs off the bar. He didn't have a chance.

"That's a trick! You're playing some foul trick on me! I want my lawyer!"

"Enough!" McGinnis closed the interrogation session. "I think we've all seen enough." He made a motion to the window of the observation room, where he knew Bartholdo was watching.

"Get him out!"

"Nooo! You idiots! She deserved it!" The insanity of Assim's words was only making the situation worse.

"I had nothing to do with this!" he yelled, vainly trying to correct himself. Savalas and the other officers already had him tight in their grips.

McGinnis was able to hear his deep voice yelling all the way down the hall, back into the holding cell.

***

McGinnis was back in his office, waiting for Lieutenant Savalas to put Assim away. The case was solved, but they were not finished just yet.

First, while waiting for the lieutenant, McGinnis picked up the phone and called his old friend.

"Pepperstone!" A calm voice responded. Every letter Dr. Pepperstone spoke was pronounced very clearly, as if read from a piece of paper in a class on diction.

"It's me, old pal!" the detective exclaimed. "Did you get the samples?"

"Oh, it's the detective again. How I adore you. Always giving me last-minute jobs just before the weekend begins."

"The case is solved, Jack. No more evidence necessary. It's only about the cake thing. It would be really good if I could verify that part of the story."

"Yeah, that chocolate cake. George went out and took a sample from the bushes. There was something sweet on there. Judging from the ingredients, it looks like it was a babka cake."

"A homemade Jewish babka?"

"Yes, Peter. Why?"

"Nothing. It's just...it's my favorite! Would've loved to get a slice. But then again, if it weren't for this case, I probably never would've met that lady anyways."

"Oh, I see. Why don't you ask Nell to make you one? She's into baking, isn't she?"

"I don't know. Maybe. She's very busy. Send that report to my email, will you?"

"Already done. Just log in and have a look. The lieutenant's got a copy, too."

*Click, click, click*... McGinnis quickly logged into his account. Indeed! As usual, his old pal was a step ahead of him, one of the few people who were.

"Here it is!"

"Yes, I know," the voice on the other end confirmed. "Do you need anything else from me, or can I finally go on my dinner date with Lydia?"

"I'm all done here, Jack. Guess I'll see you on Monday."

"Wait a minute. Not so fast, there. I can't go for dinner with Lydia without telling her who did it. After all, she might be the judge in this case, and she could stand some background information."

"That's *so* under the table Jack, but I'll tell you, because I know it's safe with you. It was the Iranian guy."

"No shit! The writer did the old lady in?"

"No, not the writer. He's as peaceful as a butterfly. His son!"

"The five-year-old?"

"No, the other one!"

"Ray West has two sons?"

"Yes, my friend, Ray West has two sons and one daughter, to be specific. But only one from a previous marriage."

"I didn't know that!"

"Of course you didn't. Ray is very secretive about his past. Nobody knew. Now you do, and I'm sure that's going to give you plenty of material to talk about with Lydia on your dinner date!"

"Do you know if his new book came out yet?"

"I don't know, man. I don't think so. I imagine there were some delays in the production plan since we mistakenly arrested his assistant for a day."

"Oh Jeez, Peter! I'm glad you have me to help you prevent such disasters. That man writes good books. I can't wait to read the next one."

"Trust me, Jack, so am I. But I have to go now. Still a lot to finish up here."

"I imagine. Don't work too hard."

"You say 'hi' to Lydia from me. And do tell me about that restaurant. Sounds intriguing."

"Will do. Bye now, ol' pal."

"Talk to you later, Jack."

# Case Closed

McGinnis was filling out his online paperwork when a knock at his office door shook him out of his computerized daze.

"Lieutenant Savalas, what a surprise! Is Mr. Esfahani safely locked away?"

Savalas nodded proudly. "Yes, he is. It was quite a struggle. Between you and me, I seriously thought he was going to knock us both down and escape, for a while."

"Glad he didn't."

"Yeah." Savalas nodded.

McGinnis confirmed Savalas' opinion of Assim. "What a monster of a man!"

"So, what's on your to-do list for the rest of the day, other than paperwork?" Savalas asked.

"Somebody should notify the West family and the other neighbors of Natalie Woodbridge's funeral arrangements, quickly. Although some distant relatives from the East Coast have been notified and even accepted taking on the cost, none of her friends from Bungalow Heaven have been informed yet. The funeral will take place on Sunday morning, at the Synagogue."

"Oh, all that totally didn't occur to me," Savalas said.

"It usually doesn't," McGinnis explained. "And that's exactly what you're here for, to learn all aspects of the job. Everybody is always so keen on finding the murderer, but nobody ever wonders what happens to the body once the person's been found."

"Makes sense to me," Savalas agreed. He had not chosen the most pleasant of all jobs. "I'll do the phone calls if you want, and take care of the paperwork after that," he continued.

"That's exactly what I had in mind for you. Oh, and do include Miss Robinson on your calling list. She asked to be notified once the details were known."

And as these words were spoken, a faint smile brightened Savalas' bruised face. The detective noticed, but as soon as Savalas became aware of it, he tried to hide it.

McGinnis politely lifted his newsboy hat as Savalas eagerly turned around, headed toward his own undersized office cubicle, where he could make the phone calls in private.

But then Savalas suddenly turned around and said: "I've got one more question, Detective."

"Go right ahead, Lieutenant!" said McGinnis.

"How did you know he would try kidnapping her?"

McGinnis played around with the rim of his hat, and unconsciously chewed on his upper lip when he was thinking, as usual. "I don't know. They all do it. Once a murderer knows that there's no way out, they start to work on instinct. Picking up a victim to shield their escape is just the next best thing to do. Only this one wasn't very consequential. He didn't know how to use her for his escape. Judging from his arrogance, it probably never occurred to him that he would get caught. But that is precisely what happened, and so when he started to feel the threat closing in, he started to act irrationally. After years of work in homicide, you develop a certain instinct and learn to anticipate the killer's actions."

"Do you think there is any chance I will ever develop such kind of instincts, Detective?"

"Just stick around, and you'll see!"

"Well, thanks a lot, Detective. Guess I'll see you on Monday."

Savalas took off. McGinnis still had a handful of work to do. Alone in his office again, McGinnis wondered whether Savalas was going to stick around. He was one of the better lieutenants he'd worked with. But if Savalas got married, like so many others, that would probably be the end of another good lieutenant in homicide. Once they had those bonds, they all left and looked for safer jobs.

***

Emma had chosen to run some errands at CVS drugstore during her lunch break on Friday afternoon. A familiar voice called out to her from across the parking lot.

"Emma? Emma Robinson?" Emma turned around to see a very pretty African American lady rushing across the parking lot, dressed in a purple mini skirt and plateau heels. Emma noticed the girl's beautiful head of brown curls swaying in the wind. When she saw that full head of curls, she immediately knew who it was.

"Adriana?" Emma asked cautiously. It was not every day that she ran into an old cellmate.

"Emma!" They studied each other carefully. It was interesting to see how much prettier both ladies looked when they were not sitting behind bars.

"I'm so happy to find you here, Emma!" Adriana began, as they gave each other a huge bear hug.

"Me, too, Adriana, me, too." On cue, Adriana's tears started rolling down her face.

"What's the matter, girl? Don't cry! After all, you made it out of jail, didn't you?"

"These are tears of joy, Emma. I'm finally *free* again. I mean, *really* free, not just from jail."

Emma looked for some tissues in her handbag, and gave Adriana the last one. Another item for her shopping list, to be purchased at CVS. She hated going there, because she always wound up buying all kinds of junk she didn't need.

"What happened?" Emma wanted to know the source of her new friend's happiness.

"I did exactly what we said I would do, the night before my court appointment. For once, I pulled together all my courage and told them the truth about the violence. I told them everything, from the very start."

"And what about the tissue box issue they arrested you for?"

Adriana snickered. This was an inside joke between the two women. She knew that Emma meant her ridiculous arrest for domestic pseudo-violence.

"It became entirely irrelevant once they saw the bigger picture. I'd love to tell you all about it one time over a cup of coffee, but I'm actually on my way to see the lawyer right now. I just needed to get some tampons."

"I see," Emma said pensively. Her night at the jail was a tough moment to recall.

"But what about you? Did you ever get the hot guy's telephone number?"

"The hot guy?" Emma asked distractedly. Adriana nodded encouragingly.

"Which one?"

Adriana giggled. "What? There's more than one?"

Emma just stared at her. She would have loved to tell Adriana about the sexy lieutenant, but it wasn't looking like there was enough time.

Adriana said: "The guy who was sneaking around your employer's property. You said he was hot."

"Oh, that one! I think he's being interrogated by the police right now."

"What, really?" Adriana was surprised.

"Yup! He is, and someone else from the property, too. But I'm not up to date about the case at all. The other day the detective visited me again, because he seemed stuck in the process of the investigation."

A faint shadow of sorrow passed over Emma's face again. It was just not fair how the old lady had been dragged into the whole affair.

"What an exciting story!" Adriana said.

"It sure is," Emma had to admit, despite her sorrow. "We definitely should get together for a ladies' night, once all this has calmed down here," Emma concluded. The two exchanged telephone numbers.

"There is someone..."

Adriana raised her eyebrows at this new information, but in that very moment, Emma's telephone rang. She looked at the display. It was a Pasadena number. This must be the detective!

"See you later," Emma whispered to Adriana, who was already dashing into the store. Both ladies were in a hurry.

"Detective McGinnis?" Emma tried to anticipate the person calling.

"It's me, George," a deep voice on the other end corrected. He purposely did not mention his title.

Emma's jaw dropped. All though they had spoken about it, she hadn't seriously expected to hear back from him.

"What...what's the matter?" Emma wanted to know. She had to pull herself together a bit. This guy was making her nervous.

"Two things. One, I thought you might like to get the information about Natalie Woodbridge's funeral."

"Yes, of course. I would like to have that," Emma said. Talking about Natalie Woodbridge made her a little bit less nervous. *The old lady is helping me with my man issues even from up above,* Emma thought.

Savalas noticed a slight hesitation on the line. "Emma?"

"Yes, I'm listening," she said.

"It's on Sunday at the Synagogue. If you want to, I can text you the exact time and address," the lieutenant said.

"Yes, that would be helpful. I don't think I can remember much of anything, right now. I'm returning to work in a few minutes, and that usually causes me to forget everything else."

Emma was doing a great job of deflecting her emotions. It was her specialty, always being very matter of fact, never exposing even the hint of a feeling. It made her feel safer and stronger, on the surface. Inside, she was jumping.

"What's the second thing?" she whispered and took a deep breath.

"Us!" The lieutenant responded very clearly and affirmatively.

"Us?" Emma couldn't believe Savalas would talk to her so directly. He had the right type of courage.

"Yes, us, Emma. I enjoyed our lunch the other day, and I would like to repeat it. Or don't you want to see me anymore?"

The lieutenant made her smile. He had charm. "Yes, of course I want to see you again," she admitted.

"Watcha doin' on Saturday? You want to go out on a real date?"

Savalas was a hero in the true sense of the term. He confronted dangerous villains to protect his fellow citizens, yet he spoke from his heart when it was called for.

Emma was thrilled. Savalas was keeping his promise. He wanted to see her for real.

"Yes, of course. What...type of thing do you want to do?" Now that she knew that his word could be relied on, she felt safer in her heart again. She might also get some information about the case. And this time, it was *her* turn to ask all the questions!

"We can have another dinner if you like, and take it from there. Meet you at your house at eight?"

"Yes, sure."

"See you on Saturday."

They hung up. Emma took a look at her watch. It was a quarter to one. She had to hurry into the CVS store, if she was going to be back at Ray's office on time.

She rushed through the aisles and grabbed all the household items on her list, including a tissue box, and hurried to the cash register.

An Asian lady with long, black hair, covered with costume jewelry from top to bottom, served her. All the employees of this store were awkward, but this lady topped them all. Her nametag read Adelaide. Emma seemed to pass by her each time she went to the store.

Adelaide always managed to wring a smile out of Emma's overly pensive face. The lady's jewelry themes were fascinating, to Emma. Today her theme seemed to be the color red, which was used in her hair ornaments, red feathered barrettes, her earrings, her necklaces, and on all ten fingers, each of which was decorated with one to three rings, all fake but fantastic. Her manicure featured a rather exquisite elaboration of red and gold nails .

*If she spent less on all that phony jewelry, she could maybe save up and buy something real one day*, Emma thought. Of course, Emma would never say these things out loud. Many people's lives would probably be a lot less cheerful if it weren't for this kooky lady's particular style.

"Oh gosh, I love your jewelry today, Adelaide," Emma told her as the Asian lady was in a hurry to scan up all Emma's items. She knew Emma a little, and that Emma was always in a hurry. She stopped just long enough to smile at Emma. She said, "My theme today is red, the color of love," and continued to scan the items.

Of course, Emma was entirely confused by now. "Oh, well, I love your fingernails, I'm always so impressed by how you can work with those long nails," Emma said carefully, deflecting the topic of love once again.

"It takes practice, darling, "Adelaide explained. "Paper bag?"

Emma considered and answered, "Yes, please." Before Emma knew it, Adelaide had stuffed all her items into the bag.

"Here you go!" Adelaide handed Emma the paper bag. Then she added, "Get yourself a nice guy. Life is short. A pretty girl like you shouldn't waste it, living without love."

Emma felt a bit embarrassed. Talking to these people in the shops felt like talking to her parents.

"Well, maybe," Emma said. She did not know what else to say.

"Have a good day," Adelaide wished her.

"Thank you!" Emma replied, and quickly rushed out of the store.

She had just enough time to walk back up Wilson Street, drop the bag off at her house, and head to Ray's office.

***

Ray was in a somber mood. Finding out that his son was the murderer had been the confirmation of his worst fear—that Assim's conversion to the American way had been merely superficial. Improving his battered relationship with Ray was just a farce, to get closer to his money and destroy his values as a peacemaker. But nobody could destroy his values, Ray knew that. He had experienced too much antagonism all his life to let this 'known' problem get any closer to him than necessary. At least, that's what he told himself.

Kate was going to have a culture shock when she returned from work. It would be necessary to discuss what to tell their children, if anything at all. Having Assim do the property management work had been Ray's way of seeking peace in his distraught family situation, but now it was all broken again. It would remain irreparable for many years. The tragedy had found its channel of the karmic continuum, despite all the efforts Ray made at spreading a message of peace. That made coping even harder than it already was.

Ray was just about to type out a general statement for the press when Emma walked in the room. God bless her patient soul. She was the angel he needed to appease this catastrophic situation again.

"What's the matter, Ray? You look pale," Emma said, and noticed that he was sitting at her place, which he never did.

Ray quietly got up.

"It was Assim," he informed her. Emma stared at him as if she didn't understand English.

"They arrested him for killing Natalie. For a while it was only a suspicion, but it's official now. Assim did it! Maureen made a video that proved it. They called me to let me know before the press."

Emma just stood there and stared at Ray's empty face. She watched his expression change gradually from nothing to total heartbreak. She had never seen him like this before.

Within seconds, Ray was tearing up and sobbing. Emma made good use of her new pack of tissues. She was reminded again why she liked working for this man, and not for anyone else. Even though he could be described as quite stubborn and difficult at times, Ray was a sensitive human being at the core. The fact that he was able to cry in front of an employee, a woman, only showed her what kind of stuff he was made of. She was proud to be his assistant.

It was only for a short moment, until he pulled himself together again. "Thank you, Emma. We have to create a statement for the press. By Monday, at the latest, they will be all over me about my family history."

"What about the *Thoughts*?" Emma wanted to know.

"We're going to use it!" Ray decided. "If anyone has any questions about my ideology, they will be referred to *Thoughts*. How much more until its completion, Emma?"

"I don't know how many more notes you have, but I have enough material to fill a two-hundred-fifty-page book right now."

"That's plenty!" Ray said. "We don't have to put it all in one book. We can do several. *That* will keep them busy, whoever is interested in this at all."

Despite all the bad news about Assim, it was good that the first volume of *Thoughts* would be printed soon.

So, Emma would be busy for the rest of the afternoon. That was good, too, because when she thought about Saturday, she got all stirred up.

# Date with a Suspect

It was late Saturday morning, and Emma was still in bed.

Work with Ray had been intense on Friday. They had tried to finish up as much as possible.

Emma's job for the weekend was to put together the first version of the compilation of *Thoughts*, so that he could finally submit it to the publisher.

Even though she had Ray's project to focus on, Emma's thoughts kept wandering to her evening date with Savalas. The fact that she did not know what to wear caused her some distress. By mid-afternoon, despite the considerable amount of work she had managed to get done, her nerves were jumping. She had to do a crash-test fashion show in her bedroom to resolve the wardrobe problem, once and for all.

The fashion show took a while. With her stubborn suits, jeans, and t-shirts mentality, she was not prepared for dating. *As a matter of fact, my wardrobe could use a general overhaul,* Emma realized, searching through her closet. Not that her closet was empty: on the contrary, it was filled up to the brim. She just wondered how on earth she had wound up with all these weird clothes. Yes, she had bought some of them herself. Some she had inherited from her best friend back in New York. Others, like a white Angora wool sweater that felt like the fur of a cat, a close friend from Australia had left her as a thank you for letting her stay at Emma's place when she had come to Los Angeles for a visit. Yes, she would like to wear that sweater tonight. But Emma wondered if it would be too hot. Also, she had no idea what to wear on the bottom. The ideal thing would be something in velvet, to match the cozy feel. *Do I have anything like that?* Emma searched and searched. While she was going through the pile of useless clothes, she remembered that someone had once given her purple velvet pants.

*Who on earth wears purple velvet, Abba?* No way. It had to be black or nothing.

Yes, Emma did have something in velvet: a black velvet dress, an inheritance from her mother's wardrobe. It was also slightly awkward. If it hadn't been for the simple belt made out of rhinestones sloppily wrapped around the hips (its only saving grace), this dress would have looked like a rag, although it was designed by Donna Karen.

But that's exactly what designers did. They copied the most outrageously dressed people from the streets, using even more outrageous fabrics, and sewed their nametags on it. There it was, finished as a designer piece. Emma didn't think much of it. The same effect could be achieved in a good second-hand store, especially the ones in Los Angeles.

Nobody could ever tell the difference between a piece of second-hand or good knock-off designer clothing and an original.

But today, she was going to wear an original by the designer Donna Karen. And the good thing was that Savalas would never know. The only thing he needed to do was like it. Emma hoped that this dress would serve.

***

Savalas spent half of his day finishing up paperwork; the other half, he spent at his apartment, waiting. He was a patient person, and he didn't get too nervous about women once he'd made up his mind about them. The bruise on his face did give him some reason for concern, though. But there was not much he could do about that. Fortunately, it was only temporary.

Nevertheless, time went by slowly, and he found himself sprucing up more than he'd planned. By the time he was ready to go, he was wearing anthracite slacks with a new polo shirt, he was freshly shaven, and his hair was gelled up like he was a Backstreet Boy. He had put on aftershave, but he didn't want to overdo it. Besides, his entire body already smelled fresh with the shower he had taken, the gel, and the shaving cream. No need to mix in any extra smells. If she liked him, she was going to like him the way he was—and that, with or without shiner.

Before he drove to Emma's house, Savalas made a stopover at a flower shop and bought a bouquet of red roses. He was serious about her, and he wanted her to know.

Finally, ready for their first real night out, he got into the car and maneuvered toward Bungalow Heaven. He parked in front of Ray's house and crossed the front lawn to Emma's cottage. He was cradling the roses in his arms as if they were a baby.

He knocked on the door and waited. Barely audible, he heard steps shuffle across a carpeted floor. *She must be barefoot*, he thought.

Emma opened the door and for the first time, she saw Savalas in civilian wardrobe. She was smitten. Of course, she immediately noticed the gigantic shiner.

"Oh my, what only happened to you?" She asked, concerned.

Savalas was immediately taken by her sexy outfit, which was so out of character for the innocent Emma.

"Occupational hazard," he quickly brushed the matter off and handed her the flowers. Emma's face broke into a huge smile. Then she took a deep breath. "Roses?" They smelled wonderful. Savalas nodded firmly.

"Careful about who you're spoiling, Lieutenant," Emma joked. "I might expect these on a regular basis."

Savalas was pretty sure he was on the safe side now and no longer saw any reason to worry about his bruised face. "Not a problem with me!" he assured.

She smiled from ear to ear and placed them in the same spot as before. The other flowers had wilted, in the meantime.

"Let's go!" she said.

Emma slipped into her ballerinas, grabbed a velvet handbag that matched her dress, and walked out the door.

***

"So how was our first real night out?" Savalas leaned over her shoulder as she searched for the keys in her handbag. He was holding her around her hips. Emma was slightly tipsy from the red wine, but enjoyed the closeness and the warmth of his breath on her neck.

"I enjoyed it," she said in a nonchalant tone, which was typical for her, then giggled. She didn't like to be pinned down.

Savalas made her turn around. He lifted her chin so she would look him in the eyes. Then, he slowly let his hands move down her arms, sliding them behind her lower back, where they stayed for a while. The lieutenant's slow moves were giving her goose bumps.

"How much did you enjoy it, exactly?" he wanted to know. Again, he leaned in to her, but this time, his body didn't stop. His longing face moved closer to hers until their lips touched, and they kissed.

Still, no answer.

***

"So?" he wanted to know, first thing the next morning. He was lying beside her, and had kissed her awake. "How much, exactly, did you enjoy it?" Savalas insisted stubbornly, as he continued to kiss her all over her body.

"A lot!" Emma declared.

Savalas' cellphone rang.

"Who on earth is calling you so early in the morning? Mommy?" Emma teased him, as she started kissing him back.

Savalas had no idea, but something was telling him it was not his mother. He got up and grabbed his phone from Emma's living room table. He took a sniff of the roses. *Wow! There's a reason red roses symbolize love.* The scent was overwhelmingly beautiful.

"Good morning, Lieutenant. Sorry to disturb you so early, but I'm afraid we have another case."

"Seriously? Now?" Savalas questioned. He was frustrated. That was going to be the end of his romantic weekend with Emma.

"Yes, Lieutenant. Dead body in the creek. Bullet in the head. Female. Blonde."

"Oh no, not another blonde. You need me to come to the crime scene right now?"

"That would be helpful. I wouldn't bother you on a Sunday morning, but I'm afraid that my Ford Futura finally died, and I need somebody to show up at the site. The address is 561 Woodland Drive."

"Sierra Madre?" Savalas asked.

"Yes, how did you know that?"

"There is no Woodland Drive in Pasadena. Only Woodland Road. Had to study those maps when I was still working as a taxi driver, back when I was a student at the academy."

"Good to know that you're so savvy with roads. My car broke down on New York Avenue at the Eaton Canyon Reservoir. I'll be getting a ride from the tow truck."

"Don't you want me to pick you up? I'm passing by there anyway."

"Thanks, but I have to wait for the truck, and somebody needs to show up at the site on my behalf ASAP. Better you go there directly."

"As you wish, McGinnis. I'll see you in a bit." Savalas hung up the phone. This is not how he imagined his weekend with his new girlfriend would go down. He got dressed.

"You have to go?" Emma asked sadly. She got up, too.

"They got a case up in Sierra Madre. Another blonde, apparently. Got to get there ASAP. McGinnis got stuck on the road."

"Sounds like he should maybe get a new car," Emma chuckled.

Then she turned serious. "So is that the last I am ever going to see of my amazingly handsome lieutenant?"

She leaned in for a kiss that was immediately granted.

"No way, Emma. If you don't mind, I'm gonna make you my very personalized blonde case, with no press involved, no detectives, unlimited dating perks, and no endings."

"I think I would like that," Emma smiled, and she passionately kissed him goodbye.

***

From that day on, Emma Robinson's life was no longer boring, or solitary.

# About the Author

Faye Duncan is a German-American writer. She is not only an avid reader of Classical American and International literature, but she was considered a walking movie dictionary for years, until she decided to move to the United States to learn more about story. Here, she has been working in entertainment for over ten years, in one way or other.

When Faye became a mom, she gave up working on movie sets with 12 to 14 hour workdays and started reading scripts for an international screenwriting competition where she not only learns a lot as a writer, but where she can be more available for her son.

Faye Duncan has a preference for writing novels, but she also has a whole stack of features, mostly in the mystery/romance/comedy genres, in development.

For more info about Faye Duncan, visit www.fayeduncan.com or send an email to info@fayeduncan.com.

# Coming Soon

## *Canyon of Shame*

Detective McGinnis is finally enjoying a week end off with his girlfriend, when the Chief of Police rings him out of bed on Sunday morning: a young blonde was found dead in a canyon creek in the small town of Sierra Madre. Unfortunately, his car breaks down on the way to the crime site, so he has to hand over the initial investigation to his partner, the good looking and savvy Lieutenant Savalas...

CPSIA information can be obtained
at www.ICGtesting.com
Printed in the USA
FSOW01n0707270716
22974FS